# "What are you trying to do, Nick?

"Take my daughter from me?" Suzannah sounded desperate.

"Make that *our* daughter," he said, catching hold of her as she tried to whirl past him. "I didn't send any letter to your father. But I know exactly what was in it. You can't get away with any more lies." He ignored her moan. "I have irrefutable proof Charlotte my child. You know it. I know it. Now your father knows it. Plus the person who devoted their time to exposing the truth for their own ends."

"I'm supposed to believe that?" The breath shook in Suzannah's throat. She jerked her arm away and moved into the living room, turning to confront him.

"You believe what you *want* to believe," he said harshly. "It's a handy trick hiding from the truth. Keeping quiet. Saying nothing. Ultimately, however, the truth will out. Charlotte is my child and I'm here to claim her."

**Margaret Way** takes great pleasure in her work and works hard at her pleasure. She enjoys tearing off to the beach with her family on weekends, loves haunting galleries and auctions and is completely given over to French champagne "for every possible joyous occasion." Her home, perched high on a hill overlooking Brisbane, Australia, is her haven. She started writing when her son was a baby, and now she finds there is no better way to spend her time.

## Books by Margaret Way

HARLEQUIN ROMANCE®
3507—BERESFORD'S BRIDE
3532—GABRIEL'S MISSION
3540—BOARDROOM PROPOSAL
3551—MAIL-ORDER MARRIAGE

HARLEQUIN SUPERROMANCE®
762—THE AUSTRALIAN HEIRESS

# Claiming His Child
## Margaret Way

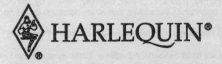

TORONTO • NEW YORK • LONDON
AMSTERDAM • PARIS • SYDNEY • HAMBURG
STOCKHOLM • ATHENS • TOKYO • MILAN • MADRID
PRAGUE • WARSAW • BUDAPEST • AUCKLAND

ISBN 0-373-03571-3

CLAIMING HIS CHILD

First North American Publication 1999.

Copyright © 1999 by Margaret Way Pty., Ltd.

This edition published by arrangement with Harlequin Books S.A.

® and TM are trademarks of the publisher. Trademarks indicated with
® are registered in the United States Patent and Trademark Office, the
Canadian Trade Marks Office and in other countries.

Visit us at www.romance.net

**Printed in U.S.A.**

# CHAPTER ONE

THERE is nothing quite like the moment of premonition. The certainty out of nowhere. The mind's acceptance. So unscientific he thought, yet he knew the instant Bebe, his secretary, breezed into his office shuffling through the pages of the latest edition of *Preview*, the luxury real estate magazine, what would be in it.

"Damn you, Suzannah," he thought. "Damn you for reaching back into my life."

"I think we'll find what we're looking for here, Nick," Bebe was saying with satisfaction, her eyes still glued to the glossy full-colour pages. Bebe Marshall, forty-eight, cheerful, enthusiastic, marvellously efficient, fiercely loyal. With an invalid mother to look after she had risked making the shift with him from Ecos Solutions when he had broken away four years ago to set up his own firm of information technology consultants. Konrads. Neither he nor Bebe had ever looked back. He was a millionaire many times over, Bebe had full-time professional home care for her mother and was now rich enough not to have to pursue work at all. In fact every other member of his team, all under thirty-five, all highly qualified, all gifted, sharing his broad vision were handsomely remunerated for their unswerving loyalty and dedication to his projects. Konrads had put itself on the map initially by creating a computer program, which greatly sped up the process followed by pathologists in the analysis of genetics and DNA testing. His current project worked on by all his staff in collaboration, was the creation of a worldwide

data base contributed to by medical specialists all over
the world, compiling and continually upgrading information relating to all aspects of genetics including DNA
testing and the classification and trends of genetic mu-
tations. It was important all-consuming work, which
would benefit not only the medical field but the legal
process and the law.

His brainchild.

"Hey, what's up?" Bebe suddenly became aware of a
certain hollowness in the silence. It was quarter to eight
in the morning. She had come in early herself to clean
up her workload but as usual Nick was already at his
work station. "Don't you ever sleep?" She fixed him
with an eye half motherly, half yearning.

"Bebe, darling, I work here. You know that. Besides
I don't need a lot of sleep. Never did." Nevertheless he
stood up and squared his wide shoulders in readiness for
what was to come.

"I suppose that's what comes of being a genuine genius." Bebe just clucked and shook her head in wonderment. Nick Konrads was *amazing*. The glowing power
source. The man who dominated all the rest, and there
were some brilliant people on his staff. Every last one of
them with a Masters degree in computer science and information technology. She blessed the day she had ever
laid eyes on him, fresh from university, fabulous brain,
with Groszmann from Ecos always trying to pick it. Not
that Nick put up with that situation long. He had every
attribute it took for outstanding success. A computer wiz-
ard, mathematician, commanding presence, an electro-
dynamic personality that made people follow him like a
messiah, yet inspired an enormous camaraderie. Everyone at Konrads felt privileged to be there. Nick was a
great boss. He involved them all in important work. He

deserved his glittering career though some in the business were bitterly envious of his meteoric rise. Nick soared above it. A man with wings. And a man who worked under tremendous pressure. Which brought Bebe back to the reason why she had bought the latest edition of *Preview*. Nick was in need of a retreat. Some beautiful quiet place he could withdraw to to relax and entertain his friends. It was she who had touted the idea, gratified and pleased when Nick had decided to go along with it.

"So tell me," he now invited, walking to the window wall with its spectacular views over Sydney and its magnificent glittering blue harbour. "Just what properties are you going to show me?" He spoke casually, even teasingly. He was fond of Bebe, but his mind and body were resonating with memories. Memories down the years from when he was a boy of ten and his immigrant mother and father had gone to live in the peaceful and prosperous country town of Ashbury in northern New South Wales. He himself had been born in Vienna of a German father and a Czech mother but his parents had brought him to Australia at the age of five. A new Australian they were then called. His father had been ill even then, both parents political refugees, though it had taken him a long time to find that out. Australia was the other side of the world. A country of great political and social stability. The only continent on earth that had never experienced the terrible bloodshed and upheaval of war on its own soil.

"Say, what's wrong with you this morning?" Bebe was soaking up the mood with an antenna of her own. "You don't seem to be listening at all."

"I am. I promise." He turned his head to smile at her, the flash of his beautiful even teeth breaking up the smouldering dark austerity of his handsome features. He was commandingly tall so Bebe, not short herself, had to tilt her head to look up to him, surprising something like pain, could it be grief, in his brilliant near-black eyes. Nick was a hundred times more complex than even she knew. A man who kept a lot inside himself.

"Well." She smiled, suddenly wanting to hug him. "I know I'm prattling on and you've probably been up most of the night but there are three properties I think you should take a look at. I've flagged them in yellow. A wonderful retreat in the Blue Mountains. Magnificent site. Splendid gardens or there's your own private Barrier Reef Island, mansion included and my favourite, a real classic...."

Bellemont Farm. He knew before Bebe ever got to the place's name. A searing brand on his heart. He almost said the name aloud, feeling the prickling on the back of his neck, the terrible tensing of his muscles.

"A four-hundred-acre estate about twenty miles from Ashbury," Bebe read on, unaware. "Used to be quite a successful horse operation and vineyard name of Bellemont Farm. Sounds lovely! Rolling pastures, splendid old colonial, a winding creek that meanders through the estate, eight bedrooms, five baths, separate staff quarters, stables, fenced paddocks, riding facilities, tennis court, pool, great fishing in the nearby Ashbury River. Just the place for a high-octane guy."

"You want to take care of me, don't you, Bebe?" he said, trying to shift his tone.

"Of course I do." She nodded her head twice. "You've taken great care of me. Mum and I include you in our nightly prayers." Perfectly true. Going with Nick had changed their lives.

The chiselled mouth with its clean raised edges gently mocked. "You have to make sure I get to Heaven?"

"When you set out to charm you'd have the angels eating out of your hand," she remarked, absolutely sure of it.

"Thanks, Bebe." He returned to his desk, giving her shoulder a little pat as he passed. Though his mouth still curved in a half smile his wonderful eyes were jet-black in their intensity. Whatever was wrong? Bebe was puzzled. She had rarely if ever seen Nick inwardly churning. A creature of enormous volatile energy he always held it under strict control. Bebe looked at him for a space of time then retreated quietly to the door. "Professor Morganthal's secretary confirmed his appointment at nine-thirty."

"I knew he'd come back to us," Nick said. "I'm the best one to help him."

"I'm sure he realises that now. If you want to dive into *Previews* for five minutes I can get you a whole lot more information. I know you're only young, Nick." Not yet thirty-one, she thought, to have accomplished so much. "And you're very strong but constant pressure is bad. You still need time off like the rest of us folks."

"All right, Bebe!" He feigned a meekness that sat oddly on his dark genius and made Bebe laugh. "I'll go through this when I have a chance. That's a promise. You might send Chris and Sarah in when they arrive. I need them to step up their information gathering. It's a massive job."

"Leave it to me," Bebe said briskly.

He worked on for ten or so minutes but in the end gave in, pulling the magazine towards him and opened up the pages where Bebe had flagged them. The Barrier Reef Island, an emerald oval surmounting a ring of pure white sand set down in a turquoise sea, glorious but maybe too far away, then in the centre, Bellemont Farm.

The place he had learned to love then hate, learned it
cruelly and indelibly like some poor dumb animal seared
by a brand. Bellemont Farm, home of the Sheffields since
colonial times. In his time, home of Marcus Sheffield and
his only child, his beautiful daughter, Suzannah. *Suzannah.* Would he never be free of her?

Just to murmur her name brought back a storm of emotion, anger and monstrous grief. Suzannah with her cloud
of dark hair loose from its school plait floating around
her heart-shaped face. Even as a child two years his ju-
nior, on first meeting her she had seemed so exquisite,
so beautifully dressed, so obviously pampered and privileged he had felt almost frightened of her. He remembered he had swallowed on a hard breath that had actually
hurt his chest. It had remained like that until, maddened
by his grave silence she had started pulling funny faces
at him and making up silly names to call him. Rude
names, too, though where she got them from living like
a princess with Marcus Sheffield for a father, nobody
knew. The horse crowd, his mother had said, laughing
ruefully. Suzannah's clowning had been infectious and
overnight they had become extraordinarily good friends.
After a while Suzannah began to take lessons from his
father in languages and mathematics after it was pointed
out to Marcus Sheffield that Nick's father had been a
highly regarded academic in his own country. Piano lessons, too, from his mother, a Conservatorium graduate
who had had to turn her fine talents to teaching ordinary
country children to bring in an income. Three years later
on the day he turned thirteen, his father died of a long-
standing physical condition Nick hadn't been able to
fathom, something to do with his lungs, leaving his
mother and him heartbroken and alone in a strange new
country where everyone seemed so extraordinarily, in-

explicably carefree, with substantially more money than they had.

That was how it started. Nick began to take on jobs. *Anything.* Mowing, mucking out stables, cleaning cars, premises, yards, a bit of carpentry. The foreign kid who seemed to be able to take care of everything. So workmanlike for one so young, practical, resourceful. It wasn't long after that he began to assert his natural academic superiority, to the extent he started to outstrip his teachers, all the time praying to God for the impossible, that his brilliant father, his best teacher, would come back. At least his father knew what he was all about. He could go straight to his father with the most vexing problem and his father could instantly see the solution. Even Suzannah, far more clever than she let any of her flighty friends know, had benefited greatly from having his father for a mentor. After his father died she continued to come to their modest home for her twice weekly piano lessons at which under his mother's guidance and her own musicality she excelled. He took over coaching her with her studies, the languages at which he was adept, and also in the maths and science subjects so that she, too, began to throw off her cloak of worked-at-mediocrity and shine. Both of them had gone to the Ashbury High School. Adored and adoring, Suzannah had refused to go off to one of the exclusive boarding schools in Sydney and be parted from her father.

"You, too, Nicko," she told him, violet eyes glowing. "I couldn't bear to be parted from you. We're soul mates."

It had seemed like that to him, too. She was never an honorary sister. The sister he never had. Even as children there had always been some distinction in his feelings. Feelings so innocent and pure they didn't disturb him

until he was what? Almost sixteen and already six feet
tall. After that things got terribly complicated. For him
and for Suzannah. Her father no longer seemed to look
upon him with the same patronising favour as before. He
eyed his height, the way he had filled out, his swift move
to early maturity. Over the years Nick had dedicated himself to looking out for Suzannah. Much like Marcus
Sheffield. But by the time he reached sixteen he began
to realise he was no longer looked on as suitable to be
Suzannah's best friend.

That role was for Martin White, icon of one of the
core group families in the district. Golden-haired, blue-
eyed, Martin who had done everything in his power to
make Nick's life uncomfortable. He was a "foreigner".
Martin never let him forget it, though they both knew the
animosity between them, which sometimes turned ugly,
had at its heart their love for Suzannah. Even at fourteen
Suzannah was surrounded by admirers, entranced by her
beauty and high spirits, and by her social standing as the
only daughter of the richest and most influential man in
the district.

River Road. A beautiful emerald place with magnificent old trees sweeping over the crystal clear waters of
the Ashbury River. All of the town's young people loved
to swim there, going off in groups. But he and Suzannah
preferred to be a pair. They had their favourite place,
Jacaranda Crossing, where one of the water holes was
considered too deep. But he and Suzannah swam like
fishes. He had to thank her for that accomplishment
though she had declared him a natural. They always took
their bicycles, tearing faster and faster along the river
road, riding down the narrow dirt track that led them to
their own private jade lagoon.

"Lord it's so hot!" Suzannah jumped off her bike

lightly, letting it go almost before he caught it and propped it against a tree. "I've never felt so much like a dip." She began right there and then to shuck off her school clothing, a terrible maroon-and-white check pinafore, white school blouse and tie, shoes and stockings, until finally she stood in her navy swimsuit, tall for her age, slender as a willow, her long exquisite limbs gilded from a summer sun, her small blossoming breasts thrusting against the tight, thin material.

He had seen her do this many times before yet suddenly he felt a stab like a hot rapier straight to his loins.

"Come on. What's holding you up?" She turned to laugh at him, her eyes brilliant with the anticipation of the kiss of the cold water.

He simply stood there, almost fully grown, staring and staring, not able to get enough breath around a few words of reply.

"Hey, you idiot. What are you staring at?" she cried. "Don't stand there like a dummy."

How could he not when he was soaking in her beauty and her femininity through every pore of his body. For the first time he truly knew what it was to be mesmerised by a woman. But she wasn't a woman; she was a thirteen-year-old girl. A little virgin. Her father's princess.

He came to then, stripping down to his bathing trunks and diving headlong into the water, grateful for the tingling coldness that closed over his head and the storm in his adolescent body. Suzannah was a flame. He knew that. And he could get burned. Even then he could think very clearly.

Yet there was wonderful exhilaration in his new discovery. Wonderful sport in swimming with her as if they were a pair of dolphins. Afterwards they pulled themselves up onto the sandy bank, their dark heads, an identical near black, sleek as seals.

"That was marvellous. Just what I needed." Suzannah towelled herself off quickly, passing her towel to him because he always managed to forget his.

Not surprisingly he didn't answer, taking the towel extended to him from her long outstretched slender arm. Life is never going to be the same again, he thought. Never innocent and sweet as it once was but fraught with tension. He recognised it easily for what it was. Sexual tension. He couldn't hold his feelings back. He had fallen in love.

"Nick?" she asked in such a strange voice. Not the usual glorious confidence, the self-assuredness befitting Marcus Sheffield's adored daughter.

"We won't ever come back here," he said. "Not on our own." The words were out in a spontaneous rush. The decision made.

"Oh, Nicko, it's *our* place," she said with a great wail. "I don't want to stick with the others."

"Your father won't want us to come here," he maintained.

"You can say that again!" Abruptly she laughed. "He'd kill us."

"So you know what I mean, Suzy." He looked at her, his expression barely veiled.

He remembered she stood perfectly still, fragile as a water nymph. "I'd be safer with you than anyone else in the world." Tears suddenly shone in her blue-violet eyes.

"Yes, you *are*, but I'm not going to do anything that could possibly harm you. You're a child."

"So are *you*." She flashed with anger.

"No, I'm not. I've never been a child like you and your friends are. In a way you're all the same."

"Well hell we are! I'm *different*." She advanced on him, her cheeks stained red.

"But you don't *see* what I see," he protested. "You don't feel as I do."

"I know I love you." She flipped back her silky black mane. "You're my best friend in all the world."

"Stupid baby. I swear I'm going to look after you." He turned away abruptly, unaware of the muscles that rippled like a panther's along his dark golden back.

She made the mistake of laying her hand along his bare skin. "Nick?"

"How about your clothes? Get them on," he all but barked, outraged by his body's powerful response.

"Nick, don't turn angry," she implored.

"I'm not angry. Never with you. Get a move on," he urged. "You said yourself your father wouldn't like us to be here."

"I'll be fourteen soon." Obediently she turned away. "The same age as Juliet."

"Don't be ridiculous." He tried to speak calmly, failed, and moved fast to collect his own clothes. He stepped into his trousers, zipped them, then reached for his dreary maroon shirt with the white trim. His mother had only just bought it and already it was getting too small. His father had stood over six foot three. He would be the same.

"No need to jump on me." Anger leapt in her voice. "You're not my big brother." Something else in her voice made him think she was about to cry. Suzannah cry? She never cried. Even when she came a cropper from her horse.

"Ah, Suzy, come on. I never meant to upset you," he relented.

"Well you have. I don't like anything about this being an adult. I don't understand what it's all about."

*Until today.*

It was then that he kissed her. Wrapping his hands around her small gilded face, touching her mouth with his own. It tasted so fresh and sweet, the shimmering joy that was Suzannah.

When he released her she held onto his wrist, the rosy delicacy of her lips pouting about to form words. Words that never came because an angry young male voice smote their ears, shouting, quivering with a kind of primal rage.

"What the hell are you up to, Konrads?" Martin White was dressed in a white shirt, jeans and sneakers, the light radiating off his thick golden hair.

He launched himself down the bank, a solid young man but no match for Nick. "Is this where you two get to?" he demanded, scarcely containing his jealousy. "Suzannah, I'm shocked at you. Wait until your father hears about this. Do you let this guy paw you?"

For answer she leapt into action, fists bunched, throwing her arm and hitting Martin squarely on the shoulder. "This guy here," she yelled, "is worth any ten of you. He's far and away the cleverest boy we've ever had in this town and probably ever will. He's not only clever he's highly principled and hard working. His father, the other kraut, was a distinguished man. His mother is a beautiful, talented lady. She plays the piano wonderfully. You're the pathetic ignoramus with your offensive name-calling. Heck, you couldn't even read until you were six. I could read when I was three!" She was so angry she was alight, pulses beating in her throat and at the blue-veined temples. "As for telling my father about anything!'' she shouted. ''Do that and I swear I'll never speak to you again for the rest of my life.''

It was a threat Martin White was to take profoundly to heart. A handful of years later he married her.

Nick's Suzannah.

# CHAPTER TWO

HEADLIGHTS coming up the driveway woke her up, illuminating the bedroom. Suddenly alert to every sound, Suzannah turned her head quickly to glance at her bedside clock: 2:35. The right side of the bed was empty, the bed linen unruffled. Martin returning home. Whatever has happened to my life? she thought bleakly. I've tried, God knows I've tried, but our marriage was doomed from the start. The lies and the heartbreak. The wounds that ran deep and wouldn't heal. She still cared for Martin even now but she had never loved him. All along Martin had known it.

The headlights didn't swerve away to the garages as she expected. Now it occurred to her the car's engine sounded different. It crunched around the broad loop of the driveway and stopped at the front porch.

She started up. The first hint of dread struck her. For quite a while now Martin had been drinking heavily. Had he been involved in an accident? Suzannah threw on her dark blue robe, thrust her feet into bedroom slippers then rushed through the open French door and out onto the upper balcony looking down.

A police car stood parked in the driveway, lights flashing.

Dear God! Suzannah whirled about almost overcome by the terrible trembling in her limbs. Was there anything more frightening than seeing a police car parked at one's door in the early hours of the morning? It could only mean trouble. Perhaps tragedy. On her flight down the hallway she paused to shut Charley's door lest her little daughter be disturbed. Her father, she knew, would be sleeping heavily. He had been taking medication since his mild stroke. She was almost at the bottom of the stairs before the door chimes rang.

"Suzannah! Terribly sorry to disturb you." It was Frank Harris, the local police chief, kneading his hat, his deputy Will Powell's kindly rugged face totally without his usual smile, two paces behind him. "May we come in?"

Suzannah stood back wordlessly, her sense of foreboding deepening with every second. She watched them move into the entrance hall with its grand divided staircase soaring to the upper level, then turn to face her ready to show their hand.

"What's wrong, Frank?" A voice came out, husky, strained. Not hers. "Is it Martin?" She could see it in his eyes.

"Mind she doesn't faint," Will Powell cried out warningly, starting forward.

Somehow they were in the drawing room, Frank gently supporting her. "I'm so sorry, Suzannah." His voice was deep, kind, distressed. He eased her into a chair. "It was an accident. Martin ran off the River Road. Piled up against a tree."

"Oh God, no!" Her whole body sagged and her face fell into her hands. No, not Martin. Life taking another tragic twist.

"I'm so sorry," Harris repeated, reminding himself there was worse news to come. Martin White hadn't been alone. His passenger had been killed as well. Cindy Carlin from the town. He had known her instantly from her long blond hair. Hell, he knew them all. Knew them from when they were kids. Suzannah, Martin, Cindy, the migrant boy, Nicholas Konrads, he had all but run out of town. On Marcus Sheffield's orders. Had to be seven years ago but he still felt terrible about it. Konrads had turned out to be a business genius. Suzannah had married the wrong man. Marcus Sheffield, arrogant, wealthy, the master manipulator had lost his substantial fortune and his once robust health. Now his son-in-law, picked by his own hand, Suzannah's husband, little Charlotte's father, was dead. For all its grandeur, Bellemont Farm, the town's historic landmark, was a sad place.

Suzannah could barely remember the events leading up to the funeral. She put herself on autopilot and somehow she got through. She never heard all the rumours and gossip that swept like a bushfire through the town. She refused help, gently turned her well-meaning friends way, explained about Daddy to Charlotte, discussed matters briefly with her father and organised all arrangements herself. Martin was gone and it was all her fault. For all that her world had fallen apart years ago.

The day of the funeral there were no tears from Heaven. Martin White was laid to rest in brilliant sunshine with family, friends, just about everyone he knew, attending his funeral at the Anglican Church where he and Suzannah had been married. It was a big funeral conducted with sombre dignity as the families closed ranks. People spoke quietly, no matter what their feelings, huddling together in groups. Cindy Carlin's funeral the day before was just the opposite with the girl's parents loud in their condemnation of Martin White and the Sheffield family who thought they still owned the town. How young Nick Konrads had been run out of town was rehashed. A great many long-standing scandals were aired.

This isn't happening, Suzannah thought as she listened to the minister drone on in what seemed to her in her grief, a mindless fashion. Her father, tall, gaunt, a shadow of his former handsome powerful self, stood by her side. Across from them Martin's family were ranged all golden haired, all distraught inwardly but steady as she was herself. Martin was to be buried in the White family plot in deference to his family's wishes. Suzannah had always got on very well with Martin's mother and sisters but they weren't looking at her now. Because of her Martin was dead. It would never be said. Just buried in hearts. The prominent families of the district stuck together. They left it to people like Cindy Carlin's family to air their dirty linen.

On the fringe of the crowd of mourners, dark glasses shielding his eyes, Nick Konrads stared at the young woman he had loved so passionately. Not even extreme tragedy could rob her of her heart-stopping beauty. Against the stark black of her wide-brimmed hat and her black suit, her skin glowed with the perfection of magnolias. He knew she had a child, a little girl, but her figure was as girlish and slender as ever, her long legs exquisite. Marcus Sheffield, her father, the man who had wrought such havoc and suffering in his life, stood protectively beside her, a striking-looking man still but his body had lost its fine shape and erect posture. Nick knew about the stroke. He knew about the failed business dealings, the downturn in Sheffield's fortunes. His agents were busy acquiring Bellemont Farm now, the scene of his humiliation. He had never thought for one moment Martin White would die an early death. No matter their tremendous differences, the way Martin and Marcus Sheffield had conspired against him, he had never wanted that. He had taken a risk, really, coming here today.

Despite the superficial changes—maturity, shorter hair, grooming, expensive clothes—many people would recognise him. But he couldn't keep away. He had received news of Martin White's death only last night, then with a wince of pain. It wasn't right, someone not yet thirty-one, the same age as himself, should be snatched so cruelly from life. How wretched Suzannah must feel. He knew the marriage hadn't been happy. He knew everything. The simple ceremony was almost over. He had to go. But nothing would interfere with his plans. It wasn't his way to hide. He would come back to this town if only as an infrequent visitor. But he could come back to this town in triumph. The new owner of Bellemont Farm, Marcus Sheffield's castle.

He would have got clean away, because he was walking swiftly to his parked Mercedes, except for Jock Craig, his old math teacher at the high school. Craig came running up behind him grasping his arm.

"Aren't you Nick Konrads? It *is* you, Nick?" His voice held surprise and an unmistakable note of respect.

There was nothing else for it but to turn and shake hands. "Mr. Craig, how are you?"

"Fine, Nick, fine." The man stared at him with keen, shrewd eyes. "Bad business, eh? A tragedy. It must have taken some courage coming back for the funeral? Although you and Martin were never exactly friends."

"Suzannah was my friend, Mr. Craig," he said, not conscious of the severity of his expression.

"Of course, of course. She's in agony, poor girl. One can see that clearly behind that ingrained poise. Actually my boy, she's coming this way. Sheffield, too. Perhaps you'd better go?" he suggested. "I only say that with the best of intentions."

"I know." Nick nodded briefly. "But Marcus Sheffield doesn't bother me any more."

"He did once." Jock Craig spoke kindly. He had never believed for one moment young Konrads was a thief, though Sheffield swore he had stolen a safe full of jewellery, which eventually turned up in the toolshed behind the Konrads' modest house.

"Sheffield has had to live with what he did." Nick's face showed nothing, neither anger nor hatred. I'm ready for him this time, he thought.

Jock Craig shuddered. He couldn't help it but Marcus Sheffield was way past dealing with anyone let alone the striking self-assured young man before him. Craig had followed Nick Konrads' career with great interest. Even as a boy he'd been staggeringly clever. Pity about the mother. Never recovered from her husband's death, the scandal about her son had almost destroyed her. Marcus Sheffield had a lot to answer for, he thought. And he wasn't the first to think it.

Nick stood quite still while she was approaching, outwardly very calm, but his tall lean frame emanated a daunting power. Inside his blood ran cold. He had loved Suzannah. Even after her betrayal and the great humiliation he had suffered, he had still yearned to see her. Proof of his obsessive attention to her lay just beneath the skin. Scratch it and draw blood. He had never recovered from her loss even when he was sleeping with other women. He had Adrienne in the car even now promising her a drive around the beautiful countryside where he had lived as a boy, with lunch afterwards at one of the fine restaurants along the coast. It was bad to use her as some kind of shield and he felt a stab of remorse. Adrienne was a beautiful woman, a divorcee a little older than he, sophisticated, charming, witty. He had enjoyed her steady

company—he was far from being a promiscuous man—
for almost a year now, keeping her friendship but not
offering anything. It seemed to suit Adrienne. Both of
them had been badly burned.

Now Suzannah approached, utterly unforgettable, her
body language taut and brittle. She was moving swiftly,
like a deer in a forest, so that her father couldn't possibly
keep pace with her. Dozens of pictures flicked rapidly
through his mind. Suzannah at all ages. The enchanting
little girl. The bewitching adolescent. Suzannah when she
had lost her status as an innocent little virgin and wept
in his arms. Natural, abundant tears of rapture and ex-
haustion. An act indelible in his memory. An act that had
wrecked his life.

Get away from here, he thought. Just get away. You
have total control over your life. This fixation on
Suzannah Sheffield. Suzannah *White* was just too bizarre.
Too damaging. He wasn't over it yet.

Suzannah, moving over the thick emerald grass without any thought to possible grass stains on her expensive
black suede shoes, couldn't have known that. The man
before her in his black funeral clothes, a long impeccably
tailored topcoat with his beautifully cut suit, looked re-
mote and unfathomable. A man whose severity of expression precluded passion. Yet how splendid he looked,
how compelling. The uncanny old telepathic thing wasn't
working. She couldn't pick up a thing. Yet why had he
come here like this?

"Nick." She reached him, lifted her head and spoke
in a clipped voice that was as cool as crystal.

"Suzannah."

His response was a faint rasp on dark velvet. He still
hadn't lost all traces of his accent. Probably never would.

"May I offer you my sincere sympathy," he said. "You must be greatly shocked and distressed."

"Traumatised, I think." Her violet-blue eyes looked away. "What are you doing here, Nick? You must know it's only asking for trouble."

If anything his striking features grew tougher. "You mean your father?" He gave her the faintest grim smile. A travesty of the beautiful one she remembered. "I really don't think your father will present a problem ever again." His eyes at that moment were full of knowledge.

"Did someone tell you we'll be moving out of Bellemont?" she asked sharply.

"No," he lied.

"Things have gone badly for us."

"You've had offers for the property?" He looked down at her, concealing all his old fascination.

"I suppose there's no harm in telling you." She gave a weary shrug. "Negotiations are going on right now. Not as much as we hoped but we're in no position to hold out."

"How the mighty have fallen," he said. "I don't think the new owner or owners would pressure you to move out in a hurry. Given the circumstances." He spoke with a kind of compassion.

"Who told you about…Martin?" Looking at his mouth as he spoke she could almost taste his lips. It caused her bewilderment and grief.

"I really don't recall who mentioned it," he said. "Bellemont Farm is an historic property, after all! Your father has changed greatly, hasn't he? He really shouldn't be leading a battle charge in his condition."

"What condition?" Suzannah asked. Was it possible he knew all about their lives? He was a powerful man.

"I was just speaking to Jock Craig." His eyebrows

raised. He'd let her believe Jock had been the one to tell him about the stroke.

Suzannah glanced behind her, apprehension in her eyes. ''It might be wise, Nick, if you left.''

He followed her gaze to where Marcus Sheffield was determinedly negotiating the grassy slope, righteous wrath all over his face. ''Actually that had been my intention only for Craig. In any case it's too late. Your father, stroke or not, is obviously determined on some kind of showdown.''

''He wouldn't forget himself on a day like this,'' Suzannah said, a little catch in her throat. ''And in such a place.''

''I think, Suzannah, your father hasn't changed much. It fills him with fury to see his beloved daughter within a foot of me.''

Once they had stood shoulder to shoulder, Marcus Sheffield had been a big man, now he was half a head shorter and stooped. ''What the devil are you doing here, Konrads?'' he snarled. ''Haven't you learnt to keep away from my daughter?''

Nick bowed slightly, his elegance quite natural. ''As pleasant a greeting as I could ask for,'' he answered, his tone sardonic. ''I believe it was Suzannah who approached me. I had no intention of intruding upon your grief.''

''So why are you here?'' Marcus Sheffield scowled, his breath shaking in his chest.

''I knew Martin for years. We grew up together.''

''He was light years away from you.'' Marcus Sheffield drew his steel-grey brows together.

''I could never understand why you couldn't see that,'' Nick retorted. ''I won't add to your distress, Mr. Sheffield. Fear of another stroke must be a worry.'' He turned to Suzannah with terrible power and grace. "Once again my sympathies, Suzannah. It was never in any of our minds Martin should die so young." With that he walked away, his long legs easily covering the distance to where a big late-model Mercedes was parked.

"Why the hell should he blow back into our lives?" Marcus Sheffield furiously demanded of his daughter. "Did you see him! Arrogance of the devil. The scorn in those black eyes."

"Don't upset yourself, Father," Suzannah murmured, looking pale and sad. She took his arm.

"The hide of him!" her father fumed, high colour mottling his cheeks. This was his first taste of Nicholas Konrads' power, and the terrible loss of his own.

"We did grow up together, Father," Suzannah said in a quiet nostalgic voice. "Nick always did have a compassionate heart. I believe he's truly sorry about Martin."

"Bah, they were never friends," Marcus Sheffield scoffed.

"That all had to do with me," she said, assuming the blame and the guilt. "Then you played your part." It was the first time she had ventured to say it.

"Everything I did was to protect you," Marcus Sheffield pronounced stoutly.

Suzannah couldn't answer, a cascade of tears fell down her heart choking her. Her father was speaking the truth as he saw it, a truth that had blown her life apart. Because of her father, his powerful influence and her unquestioning belief in his integrity, she had become more deeply entwined with Martin, then a short time after the furore of Nick's disgrace and departure had abated, married him in the same church from whence he had been buried.

Demons would pursue her all her life. Memories. The pain and the bitter betrayal in Nick's brilliant eyes. The

agony in his mother's. The triumph in Martin's and her
father's. They had won. In their way they had kept her a
prisoner while Nick was shipped off with his long-
suffering mother.

Suzannah wondered how she could ever have believed,
even for one wavering moment, that Nick was a thief.
Nick the hero of her girlhood. Wonderful, sweet, kind
with the magic and power of a white knight. How had
she ever allowed her father and Frank Harris to convince
her he had stolen anything from the safe? So he knew
the combination? He had been with her when she put her
good pearls away. Nick noticed everything. Money had
been very tight in the Konrads' household, never more
than after Nick's father had died. Mrs. Konrads, not a
strong woman after experiences she would never talk
about, had had to work too hard, taking domestic jobs in
the homes of the wealthy to help out. Nick had adored
his mother. He could scarcely contain his anxieties about
her, longing for the day when he could support her properly. The day that never came.

Suzannah's own anguish was permanent and deep.
People were following. There was to be the ritual gathering at the house. Nearing the car, an old but beautifully
maintained navy Rolls, they saw Nick drive away. In the
passenger seat, looking out with intense interest was a
very good-looking woman with short bright chestnut hair,
fine regular features, designer sunglasses perched on her
nose. Just a few seconds, yet Suzannah caught the flare
of her nostrils, the intensity of the stare that was directed
solely at her.

Nick's wife? She had read about him in the newspa-
pers from time to time, seen pictures of him and various
glamorous women companions in society magazines, but
she had never read a word about his getting married. Not

that that meant anything. Nick always had been a very private person.

Who could not fall in love with him?

Sadness seeped into her steadily. Her early womanhood had been swept away. She had bowed to intense pressure. She had bowed to a concerted barrage of lies. She had lost Nick and deserved to. She had lost Martin who had asked for nothing but the love she couldn't give him. Charlotte was the only one to call her back to Bellemont. Her adorable dark-haired little daughter. So much like her. Except for the eyes.

Inside the Mercedes, Adrienne made a big effort to keep an uncontrollable spurt of jealousy out of her voice. "Who are these people, Nick? Did you know them well?" She took off her sunglasses, and turned her spectacular amber eyes in his direction. Things weren't going half as well as she had hoped with Nick Konrads. They always had a good time. He appeared to enjoy her company—she knew there wasn't anyone else—but in the end their relationship wasn't flowering. She was desperately in love with him. Had been in love with him from the moment she laid eyes on him for that matter. He was simply *extraordinary*, but so complex even now she didn't feel she knew the least thing about him. She did know however he wasn't in love with her. She wasn't such a fool she didn't realise that. But they communicated very well on the sexual and social level. She and a woman partner ran their own successful public relations firm. Nick admired hardworking successful people. God knows he was the man of the moment. Businessman of the Year.

Who was that young woman he was speaking to? Although they stood a couple of feet apart, it seemed to Adrienne's tormented eyes their bodies were almost straining towards each other. Surely an illusion? The shimmering, dancing light of the sun.

Nick took his time answering, aware of Adrienne's powerful curiosity, the jealousy that shone in her eyes. "We all knew one another when we were growing up. Martin White, it was his funeral, was my age. His widow, Suzannah, was a friend of mine."

"Suzannah? The woman you were talking to?" She had always felt there was someone in the background. Some shadowy figure.

"Suzannah Sheffield, that was."

She took a moment to digest this. "Sheffield? Isn't there a historic homestead around here someplace? Used to run sheep, then turned into a horse breeding establishment when wool took a dive? The name of the place is on the tip of my tongue." She resisted the impulse to crease her forehead.

"Bellemont Farm," he supplied quietly.

"Yes, of course." Adrienne suddenly hated the slender young woman in her widow's weeds. "Didn't I see somewhere it's on the market? I take all the usual magazines."

"I believe it is," he answered casually, curiously unwilling to take her into his confidence. "We can skirt the property if you like. Impossible to see the house from any of the roads. It's a long drive from the front gate and the house is nestled in a grove of jacaranda trees. It's a glorious sight when the great trees are in flower."

"Sounds like you knew the place well?" Adrienne flashed a glance at his handsome profile.

"Every inch of it. Suzannah used to take me over it when her father was away on his polo weekends."

Something in his voice gave off shivery little sparks.

"That sounds like you weren't allowed there when he was?"

"You're so right." His tone held the weight of dislike. "Marcus Sheffield was and remains the biggest snob in the world."

"And Mrs. Sheffield?" Nick could twist *any* woman around his little finger.

"She ran off when Suzannah was barely four," he told her. "One of Sheffield's opponents on the polo field, would you believe? They went to live in South America. There was no question of her getting custody of Suzannah. Marcus Sheffield was establishment. A very powerful and monied figure. He adored Suzannah. His only child. He was very bitter about his wife. Her name was never permitted to be mentioned."

"That must have been terribly hard on your Suzannah," she said a little harshly.

He did glance at her then. A penetrating look. "Her father never gave her time to miss her mother too much. He doted on her. Couldn't bear her out of his sight. For that matter Suzannah was devoted to him. She was too young to see he ruled her life."

Adrienne tried to give a little understanding laugh; she did not succeed. Suddenly she was afraid she couldn't hold onto Nick Konrads much longer. She had felt that way, she now realised, as soon as she laid eyes on this Suzannah. Nick was better than anyone she knew at hiding his true feelings, but she had seen what she had seen.

Garry Hesson, his solicitor, rang him. "All sewn up, Nick," he said, sounding pleased with himself. "They're allowed to stay on six months or until they relocate, according to your instructions. Marvellous place. Allow me to congratulate you. *And* beg for a visit."

"Make it a weekend," Nick responded, leaning back in his swivel chair. "Bring Jenny and the kids."

"They'd love that," the solicitor whooped. "Won't hold you up, Nick. I know you're doing great things."

Am I? In some ways, he thought, but that doesn't absolve me. How many times over the years had he envisioned bringing Marcus Sheffield to his knees? Now it was done. He owned Bellemont Farm lock, stock, and barrel. He thought it would mean a lot, now suddenly it didn't mean much at all. He couldn't get Martin's violent death out of his mind and the circumstances that had led to his having an affair with young Cindy Carlin from the town. He could just barely remember Cindy. Blond, pretty, a school drop-out, he thought. Poor little Cindy. What a terrible end. He was shocked. Martin must have been dreadfully unhappy. He had never looked at anyone but Suzannah. Challenged any of his friends who tried to get near her. Martin had sold his soul to the devil to get Suzannah, hiding the jewellery from Marcus Sheffield's safe in the Konrads' old toolshed. He must have hidden there for quite a while before he was able to gain his stealthy access. Martin, his face a white mask, accusing him of bragging about some "coup" he had pulled off. Suzannah on her feet, violet eyes flashing with the light of battle for him. The light had gone out later when her father accused him quietly and contemptuously of grossly abusing their trust.

"I wouldn't care about you, young man," Marcus Sheffield had said with icy disgust. "You could go to jail for my money. It's the place, after all, where thieves go. It's your mother I pity. Hasn't she had enough to endure?"

He remembered defending himself vigorously, offering arguments to Frank Harris the police chief, who just stood there stiffly, almost miserably, as if he were in Sheffield's employ. Finally it became starkly apparent his defence was falling on deaf ears. He was guilty. Even Suzannah never challenged her father again. She just gave up. As he did. He had stolen because he and his mother were in a precarious financial position. The ultimatum was put to him bluntly. For his mother's sake, since every piece of jewellery had been recovered, he would leave town immediately. If he was prepared to do that, no further action would be taken.

He knew all about justice even then. He had his parents' experiences as an example. Justice was in the hands of the powerful. Marcus Sheffield was the wealthiest and most influential man in the town. He owned many businesses, whole parcels of real estate. Hundreds of people one way or the other relied on him for an income. Suzannah had tried to speak to him the day that he left, begged him to meet her but he had hung up on her, white-faced and furious. In the moment of crisis the girl that he loved, that he ached with passion for, had trusted her father above him. She had actually believed he was a common thief. For weeks after she had tried to speak to his mother, weeping with frustration when his mother refused to tell her where he had gone, where he was staying. Although his mother had come to love Suzannah as a daughter, a deep well of fear and anxiety had stopped her from ever allowing Suzannah to get close to her son again. It wasn't long after that he landed his job with Ecos Solutions and his mother was able to come to him. And Suzannah, who had blazed with love for him, had married Martin White. Absurd to think of it now but he had always rated Martin's chances as next to nil. So his parents were close friends of Marcus Sheffield's? So Martin had been in love with Suzannah for most of his life? Suzannah had promised to be "his girl for all time". And poor fool that he was he had believed her.

# CHAPTER THREE

"YOU'RE very quiet, darling. Is everything all right?" Suzannah glanced away from the road to check on her small daughter riding in the passenger seat. Usually Charley chattered endlessly on their trips to school. This was their private time together free from the constraints of Marcus Sheffield's uncertain tempers and pinched moods. The reversals in their lifestyle had changed him greatly, his unhappiness exacerbated by the effects of his stroke. They were living now in one of the "cottages" Marcus Sheffield still owned, a comfortable small residence set on a quiet cul-de-sac near the river. Most people would have been very pleased to own it—it had an exceptionally beautiful garden—but Marcus Sheffield was making himself truly ill with misery. Sheffields had owned Bellemont Farm since the early days of the colony. The quality of wool from Bellemont sheep had been famous. Bellemont horses, too. The yield from their wines had been small but of great quality. Above all the property and the homestead were magnificent. Bellemont had a lot of history attached to it and Marcus Sheffield had enjoyed tremendous standing. And then to have lost it all?

"Grandpa is very cranky," Charley said and heaved a great sigh. Grandpa had thundered at her to eat up all of her breakfast. "It's really funny living at the cottage. It's such a little house. I can run from one end to the other in a minute."

"But pretty, darling." Suzannah threw her a comforting smile. We'll get used to it. We have one another."

"I'd like us to be alone," Charley said in a little voice, looking down at the hands in her lap.

"But, darling, who would look after Grandpa?"

"I'm sorry," muttered Charley.

"You have nothing to be sorry about. You're such a good girl. I know Grandpa has been speaking sharply lately but he's very upset."

"So are you but your voice is always lovely. Grandpa is just plain rude."

"I'll talk to him about it, sweetheart. It's just that he yearns to be back at Bellemont."

"So do I. It's the bestest place in all the world," Charley answered quite passionately. "I'm going to miss it when all the jacarandas are out."

"We can take walks along the river," Suzannah told her consolingly. "The road is lined with jacarandas."

"It's not the same," Charley maintained sadly. "When is this person who bought Bellemont going to move in? Is he going to live there? Does he have children? I'll bet they want a pony, but they can't have mine."

"No one is going to have your pony, Charley," Suzannah reassured her. "Lady is being well looked after. You can get to ride her at the weekend. As for the owners, I know nothing about them. The farm was bought in a company name. I'm going to take a run out there after I drop you off at school."

"What for? Won't it be terribly sad?" Charley turned huge blue-green eyes on her mother, loving the way she looked, the scent of her, the way her shining dark hair curved in under her chin. Her mother was beautiful. Everyone said so.

"It will be sad, darling." Suzannah could hardly deny it. "But we have to be brave."

"Okay." Charley leaned over and touched her mother's hand, sharing their love. "Do you miss Daddy?" she asked.

It caught Suzannah unawares. "Of course I do, darling," she said on a wave of love and protectiveness. It was unlikely Charley had been spared all the rumours at school. Small children could be cruel.

"He didn't like *me* very much." Charley pulled vigorously at her plait, her eyes darkening to jade.

"Darling, he loved you." Suzannah bit at her lip.

"Did he really?" The question sounded more philosophical than vital to Charley's interest. "He never wanted to take me anywhere. He never listened to me play the piano. He never rode with us."

"Daddy wasn't a horse person like we are." Suzannah quickly mustered an excuse for Martin's behaviour. "Besides, he had lots of things to attend to for Grandpa. Grandpa kept him very busy."

Charley consulted her mother's face again. "Grandpa said Daddy made a lot of terrible mistakes. He said some of them made us lose our home."

"He didn't say this to you, Charley, surely?" Suzannah's fine arched brows drew together.

"He said it to Mr. Henderson when he came to call."

"And where were you, young lady?" Suzannah asked quietly. Henderson & Associates was her father's law firm.

"Behind a chair," Charlie admitted. "I wanted to move but Grandpa walked into the room with Mr. Henderson. He was talking very loudly. I knew he was angry. I sort of froze."

"And you were there all the time?" Suzannah gasped.

"Until they went into the library. Grandpa said a lot of things about Daddy."

Of course Martin had made terrible mistakes. "That's because he had no idea you were there," Suzannah answered.

"He was really angry about all the…talk." Charley threw her mother an uneasy glance.

"People always talk, Charley," Suzannah said. "We must honour your father's memory and move on. Daddy did his best in a difficult situation."

"That's because he loved you, Mummy," Charley answered her.

The wattles were out all over the rolling hillsides. Golden masses of puffball blossoms, so typically Australian, the wattle was the country's floral emblem, wreaths of it entwined around the coat of arms. It was a glorious day, the scent of the profuse blossoming carried in heady wafts on the breeze. All the flowering prunus, the peaches, plums and cherries were out, too. "Roses by other names," Suzannah thought, her eyes delighted by the sight of a whole line of them decorating a white-fenced property line. Another few weeks and her beloved jacarandas would burst into bloom, hazing the hillsides in indescribable shades of mauve-blue. In Australia the flowering of the great trees means exam time for all students, most crucial to school leavers vying for a place at university. She had passed her leaving exams with flying colours, Nick with a perfect score. Both of them had attended Sydney University, Nick boarding with a couple who took in the occasional student, while she lived in at one of the university women's colleges. Both of them went home at weekends and holidays. The halcyon days when they revelled in the freedom of each other's company. She finished her Arts course first and returned

home to the father who had missed her dreadfully. Nick
continued on with his studies, a brilliant student of whom
great things were predicted.

It was when Nick was in Sydney she and Martin had
grown closer. She had known Martin all her life. He was
almost like a cousin. She was much liked by his family
whose dream was the two of them should marry. They
went to dances. They went to parties. They went to country club dinners. Suzannah never asked, but Martin always took her. He had other dates, of course, which
pleased her. Martin had only been her friend. He had
been madly in love with her. She could see that *now*. But
then he had kept the depth of his feelings under wraps,
never going beyond a quick kiss goodnight, content it
seemed to be her escort. The trouble always started when
Nick came home, so stunning, such an achiever, the girls
all raved about him. She might have been fiercely jealous
with all her friends pursuing him, only the bond between
them grew deeper and deeper, dominating their existence.

They never had sex though sex was on everyone's
mind. Courting. Pairing off. Nick continued to take care
of her. It was as simple as that. Didn't they know in their
hearts one day they would get married? But first Nick
had to gain his Masters degree after which he would be
offered the world. Such were their dreams. Dreams that
would be cruelly shattered. Her father's dream had been
vastly different. Nicholas Konrads had no part in it. Nick,
her honourable knight.

It was a long tree-lined driveway up to the house with
beautiful views of the vineyards on the hill and the deep
tranquil creek that wound its way through the entire estate. What would the new owners do with all this?
Continue the same operations? Reopen the stables, the

winery? Everything had become so terribly run down.
Heavens alone knew why her father had placed Martin
in charge. Martin had had no real head for business. He
had been nervous conducting transactions. He hadn't par-
ticularly liked horses though he drank more than his fair
share of the wine. But Martin had been one of *them*. One
of the old families of the district. Her father, astute man
that he was, had gone along with that. To his cost.

The homestead rose up in front of her. Handsomely
sited on a hilltop, it was a wonderful old colonial of mel-
low rose-hued brick with white columns soaring to the
open upper balcony, its broad terrace wrapped around
with white wrought-iron lace. There were other buildings
ranged all around it and to the rear, but the homestead
was set like a jewel in an oasis of jacaranda trees, screen-
ing all other buildings from sight. Nearing the house, the
driveway went into a loop surrounding a spectacular
white marble fountain her great-grandfather had had
shipped back from Italy. In her childhood it used to play
all the time. Now it was quiet and forlorn in the warm
sun, free of the beautiful pink waterlilies that once had
festooned the large bowl.

Suzannah stopped the car at the foot of the short flight
of stone steps, surprised to see the front door with its
splendid side lights and fan lights open. Perhaps the agent
was there? Though there was no sign of her car. Had she
parked it at the rear? Suzannah still retained her set of
keys, making the commitment that the house would be
in perfect running order for when the new owners would
arrive. Hastily she climbed the steps, putting her hand to
the door chimes, calling out the agent's name.

"Kathleen, is that you?"

Absolute silence, though now that she looked a set of
keys was in the lock. At least it wasn't a burglar, though

burglaries in the district were unheard of. "Kathleen?" She advanced into the entrance hall, staring first up the central staircase then walking into the drawing room. What was Kathleen doing if indeed it was she? Checking on the house? She didn't have to worry. Suzannah made her weekly visit even though it pained her deeply to keep coming back.

The huge L-shaped drawing room, dominated by two carved white marble fireplaces surmounted by identical Georgian giltwood mirrors, was empty. A good deal of the original furnishings had been sold with the house— the heavy antique furniture, the dining-room suite and sideboards, everything in the white-and-gold ballroom, most of the paintings, the oriental screens and rugs, the bronzes. The cottage couldn't possibly accommodate a quarter of it, let alone the grandeur. Perplexed, she found herself walking to one of the Georgian mirrors, staring at the reflection of a heart-shaped face within a frame of dark hair. It wasn't a happy face. Even her eyes looked sad.

"Suzannah?" A voice said behind her, making her heart lunge in extreme shock. She put a quaking hand to her breast, then spun sharply, pulling back her shoulders as though confronting a powerful danger.

"God, *Nick!*" Her magnolia skin lost all colour. "How can you possibly be here?" At first it wouldn't sink in, then she caught her breath as reasons absorbed her.

Nick had talked of vengeance as a soldier might swear allegiance. "I'll be back, Mr. Sheffield," he had promised as Frank Harris bundled him into the police car. "I'll be back and it will be a bad day for you."

Suzannah felt a chill like an icy hand to her forehead. "Of *course!* You bought it, didn't you? You're the new owner?" She was convinced she was right.

"My cup runneth over." He spoke sardonically though pain slashed his heart. Where was her wonderful incandescence? All gone. Yet she was never more lovely, her wonderful hair loose, body thin enough to be breakable, mauve shadows beneath her haunted long-lashed eyes.

"Why didn't we know?" she agonised.

"I didn't *want* you to know," he said, hard mockery flooding in. "That should be obvious."

"I mean why didn't we guess?" Something like anger leapt in her violet eyes. "I've always known in my heart you'd get back at Father."

"And you. Don't forget *you*, Suzannah. You're the one who told me how much you loved me. You're the one who was going to be my girl forever."

"Except fate got in the way." She wrapped her arms around herself, warding off the condemnation that flowed from him.

"You can call it fate if you like," he said, black eyes brilliantly ironic. "I'd call it treachery, betrayal and blackmail."

"You'll never forget." It made her feel desolate. Terribly alone.

"Did you think I would?"

"My father is a sick man, Nick."

He shook his dark head. "I didn't cause his stroke, Suzannah. I didn't bring his world crashing down on his head. If I didn't buy Bellemont somebody else would."

"Why would you want it at all?" she flared. "Your life is elsewhere. Your company, your career. You must be married?" That woman in his car. She'd felt seared by her stare.

"I haven't had the slightest urge to get married," he told her curtly. "Unlike *you*. To answer your question. This is a magnificent property. I'm in need of a country retreat. Somewhere to relax. Bring my friends and overseas guests.''

"A retreat?" That checked her. "You're not going to return it to a working farm?"

"As a matter of fact I am. If that's all right with you and your father," he said, freezing her out.

"You're so bitter."

"I most certainly am, but don't worry about it." He moved nearer, making her feel she was being backed into a corner. "How are you settling into your new home? I took a run past it last night. The Saunders used to be tenants, didn't they?"

"So you didn't arrive this morning." Her brain seemed to be wrapped in cotton wool.

"No, Suzannah," he explained patiently. "I drove up from Sydney yesterday. Stayed the night." In her bedroom where he had made love to her that one time. Trapped her into surrender with his overwhelming passion.

"But where did you sleep?" she asked. The furniture from the guest bedrooms had been sold. They had taken theirs with them.

"What does it matter?" In fact, he had brought a sleeping bag. Dossed down on the floor. "I might ask the questions. What are *you* doing here, anyway? On my property." This wasn't the way it was meant to be but he couldn't stop himself.

"Making sure it remains in the same condition as it was sold to you." She flushed.

"You have no obligation to do that."

"Can't you stop, Nick?" she begged, knowing nothing would heal the wounds.

"Stop what?"

"Being so hateful."

That made him smile. A flash of white teeth, no humour at all. "That's good coming from you. The fact remains, Suzannah, and nothing can change it, you accused me of being a thief."

"I *didn't.*" She had trusted her father who had never lied to her. What she had felt for Nick was an overwhelming pity.

"Your very silence condemned me."

There was no cure for injustice. "I bitterly regret it, Nick." Tears came to her eyes. Tears from a deep place inside her. "Can't you forgive me?"

He turned his handsome head abruptly. "You want the bad news? *No.* My mother died, did you know that?"

"We heard." It had come as a tremendous blow. "I wanted to write to you but I thought you would only hate me."

"I'm afraid you were right," he answered, very soberly. "She died of a broken heart."

Suzannah moved away from the fireplace, sought the French doors and opened one to admit the breeze. "I cared about her, Nick. So much."

"She cared about you."

"She would never tell me where you went."

"You should know the answer to that. She thought quite rightly you had done me enough harm. Anyway, it must have been a fleeting idea of yours. The next thing we know you married poor Martin. He must have swept you off your feet."

She had the sensation the room was swirling around her. "It made my father happy."

"And you were born to make your father happy. What about *you*, Suzy? It seems terrible to talk about it at a time like this but it's no secret your marriage wasn't a great success."

She moved slowly to one of the big custom-made sofas and sat down before she fell. "I have my daughter. I adore her."

His expression tautened. His black eyes studied her. "She could have been our child." A long pause. "What's her name?"

Colour flamed into her white face and she dropped her gaze. "Charlotte. We call her Charley."

For a moment he was at a loss to answer her, then he rasped. "Charlotte? How dare you use my mother's name."

Her own anger flowed hot and swift. "This is me, Nick, remember. *Me*. Suzannah. Your mother told me once I was the daughter she had always wanted. Through your mother I became an accomplished pianist, more valuably, a better person. I had a perfect right to call my child after a women so influential in my life."

"You expect me to believe that?"

"I do," she cried in sharp defence.

"Your father must have loved the sound of that. So must Martin."

"Neither of them knew," she said, suddenly quiet. "Your mother was Mrs Konrads. Her christian name didn't come into it. Your father called her Lotte. Father and Martin didn't see the connection."

"Come on," he jeered. He came behind her, his hands slipping onto her shoulders, holding her fast.

"They just didn't," she protested, as many emotions enveloped her. "Charlotte is a beautiful name."

He withdrew his hands instantly before he lost himself in sensation. "You must be a lot happier with Charley."

"It's just a nickname," she said in a confused voice. "She's only six. Adorable."

"Does she look like you?" he asked harshly, feeling tremendous anger for all he had lost.

Suzannah nodded. "Almost my mirror image so they tell me."

"So you fell pregnant the night you were married?" He looked down at her as she sat folded into the sofa, the vulnerable slope of her shoulders, the delicate curve of her breasts clearly outlined against her thin pale pink sweater.

She enunciated her words very carefully. "I'm not going to discuss my married life with you, Nick."

"When everyone knows it was unhappy. I couldn't believe it when I was told Cindy Carlin was with Martin at the time."

Martin starved for love and laughter. "I feel very badly about that, Nick. You can't know."

"I think I do." He forced himself to look away from her. "What I *can't* figure is why? Martin was crazy about you."

"Not for long." She shook her head vehemently.

"What is *that* supposed to mean?"

"The best way to say it is we didn't have a lot in common."

He shrugged his shoulders, their width apparent under the black polo knit. "I could have told you that a long time ago. *Why* did you marry him, Suzannah?" A question he had asked himself at least a million times.

What was she supposed to tell him? "God knows," she said, focusing on her hands. "On the rebound. Never a word from you. Your mother choosing to clam up on me."

"That happens with mothers. She was thinking of *me*. Me with my anger and humiliation. Before God I swore to get even. Your father would have had me in jail. Did you realise that? In jail for something I didn't do. It's called fabricating evidence. And Frank Harris went along with it."

She bowed her head, her dark hair falling forward like a curtain. "Father had the highest reputation." *Then*. But fear of losing her to Nick had warped his integrity. It was she who had screamed at her father in protest, actually shouted and screamed like an out of control teenager until he promised not to bring charges against Nick. If only Nick left town. That was the ultimatum. Her father was a man of action. He meant what he said. He was determined to stamp out all trace of Nick. In her life. In her heart. But there he had never succeeded. Her longings had only multiplied with the years.

"I'm so sorry, Nick. I beg you to forgive us." She lifted her heart-shaped face, drawn with pain.

He was afraid of this. The sharp ebbing of his anger. Afraid of the sheer magic of her now that she was here in front of him. "You didn't believe me then," he said harshly, "so when exactly did you learn the truth? I can't believe your father confessed. He wouldn't confess to anything even on his death bed."

It was she who had to reevaluate everything. "It was Martin," she said. Poor Martin. She felt loathe to name him. "It preyed on his mind for years. He wanted to get it out in to the open."

Nick wheeled in his pacing, thinking of Martin sneaking into their toolshed, planting the jewellery. "Of course, Martin. He probably thought you would excuse him his crime. Martin White, the golden boy of the district, doing everything your father told him, so your father would reward him with you."

"He's dead, Nick," she pointed out in a ghost-ridden voice.

"Beyond my forgiveness."

"And mine. I can't spare myself. I wasn't good for Martin."

How they were all bound together! "Martin wanted you no matter what happened." He felt an ugly surge of bitterness. "Don't take all the blame. Tell me about Charlotte, your little girl." He walked to the sofa opposite her, a look of steel replacing the sweetness he had always kept for her.

Cold wings of fear beat against her heart. "She looks like me when I was a child." Except for the *eyes*. "She's tall for her age. Highly intelligent. Too bright for Grade One. The school only kept her there a couple of weeks before putting her up to Grade Two where she easily holds her own. I've started her on the piano." She remembered vividly the way Charley had gone to the big Steinway in the drawing room and started picking out tunes at the age of three. She had started to read at that age as well. Her gifted little daughter. It was in the blood.

"And, is she interested?" he asked, waiting for her answer.

"She loves it."

"She must have inherited her musical ability from you. I distinctly recall from our school days Martin was tone deaf. I'd like to meet her." See *my* Suzannah again, he thought.

"I don't think that's possible, Nick." She turned her head away from him.

"Why? Are you still toeing the line?"

"Let's just say, I'm a prisoner of 'family.' My father is no longer a well man. I can't abandon him. Though you have every reason to hate him he has shown nothing else but love to me."

"Oh, Suzannah, wake up. Since when is love overriding self-interest? Your father wasn't interested in your happiness. He was only interested in his own. When your mother ran off and left him he turned his entire focus on you. You were perfect to adore. A beautiful, healthy, intelligent, exuberant child. You brought great pride and satisfaction into his life. It might have been different if you hadn't been attended by all the good fairies at birth."

"If I was, they soon flew off," she answered bleakly.

"But surely he doesn't think you're going to remain a widow for long or has he Martin's successor already picked out?"

She rose swiftly, her cheeks flaming, her whole body bathed in heat. "You'll have to excuse me, Nick. I have things to attend to."

"Like what?" he challenged her, following her with his eyes.

"For one thing, finding myself a job."

He gave a soft, derisory laugh. "Surely your father has a bit of money left?"

"I *want* a job," she said, almost vibrating with anger and the old fierce desire. "Part-time anyway. I have to be on hand for Charlotte."

"I could offer you the job of caretaker," he said cruelly.

"Wouldn't you *love* that?" Anger spilled from her lambent, violet eyes.

He stared at her while her colour came and went. "Did you think I *wouldn't* want to make you suffer?"

"I'm aware you have a ruthless streak in you. I'm aware you've always seen me as yours. There's too much power in you, Nick," she said. Hadn't he been with her every day of these past years, even when he had left her without a word?

"It must have dealt Martin a tremendous blow to find

you weren't a virgin?'' he suggested, turning her bone-white.

In fact Martin had had too much to drink to register anything but the enormous thrill of winning her for a bride. And it had been war. Nick versus her father and Martin.

"If he knew he never said anything about it." Strain showed itself in every line of her body.

"Especially when he was mad about you. Prepared to do anything to get you. When did you discover you were pregnant?''

"When I first threw up,'' she answered flatly, feeling decidedly queer.

"I repeat, I want to see Charlotte.'' His striking face wore an implacable expression.

"Charlotte has nothing to do with you, Nick.'' She stared at him with her black-fringed eyes. "All you can bring us now is trouble.''

Outwardly he laughed. Inwardly his mind was working furiously. "I think you're lying about something.''

"I'm going now, Nick.'' The conversation had become unendurable and she didn't know where it would end.

"One moment.'' He flung out his arm, grasped her shoulder. "What's the matter, Suzy? You look afraid of me.''

"Why not? You're about to wreck our lives,'' she burst out recklessly.

"How? No, don't struggle. Answer me. *How?*''

Her mouth went dry. "I'm putting my father's well-being above every other consideration.''

"What has that got to do with my seeing Charlotte?'' he demanded, looking so volatile his black eyes sparkled.

"You may upset her,'' she countered.

"I'm just fine around children," he scoffed. "I have two godchildren as a matter of fact. I often visit them."

Her mouth trembled and she heard herself whisper. "Let go of me, Nick. If I'd have known you were here, so totally unexpectedly, I would never have come."

"And I might never have known you have a daughter called Charlotte," he countered. "I've had my revenge acquiring Bellemont but I think on the whole I'm the one who was sinned against, okay?"

She could only nod. "I've spoken of my sorrow, Nick. Forgive me. Forgive my father. But don't let either of us ever speak again."

"That's not what I've come for," he said, verging on losing control.

Her ears roared as he pulled her into his arms, securing her wrist as he forced his mouth over hers. Her heart gave a great upward leap in remembered bliss, yet she closed her eyes in terror as all the old tumultuous passion surged through her veins.

Pain. Loneliness. Sexual starvation. They were all swept away. The years didn't count. She was back in the past, her body shuddering against Nick's, half agony, half ecstasy flaring in her stomach, her breasts, her womb, her limbs. She couldn't even manage to free her hand. He wasn't letting her go, kissing her so deeply, ardently, endlessly, and an answering desire flooded her being. She could not see the past, the future. Only now.

"Just look at you!" He shocked her badly then, wrenching his head back to stare down into her unguarded face, the pulsing half-open mouth, the shut eyes, the expression of yearning. It was all there. A ravishing homecoming. "Tell me now you don't want to speak to me again," he taunted her. "You're *waiting* for me, Suzannah. Martin's less than perfect wife."

She made to hit him then, thinking she wanted to kill him, burning with shame to the roots of her hair, attempting to strike him furiously across his beautiful sensual mouth, but his firm hand stayed her.

"So you're not completely without the old spirit." He hauled her even closer.

The world had stopped spinning, and came back into sharp focus. "That's all we ever had. Sex." It was the most ridiculous thing she had ever said in her life, but her sense of humiliation was oppressive.

"I only had you once," he reminded her, utterly unmoved by her charge. "In this house, in your bedroom." *Where I slept last night dreaming of you and your betrayal.* "The only time I knew your beautiful body. But not the last." He took hold of both her hands. "I'm going to be the man in your life, Suzannah. And there's not a damned thing you're going to be able to do about it." He smiled a grim, triumphant smile that affected her profoundly.

She found the strength to break away, hurrying to the entrance hall. "Stay away from me, Nick," she called back at him.

"I'm not going to, Suzy. You know that." He came after her, looking so powerful, so mesmeric the tears began to pour unheeded down her face. "You have this coming to you for what you did to me. You and your father might want to think about that."

When she finally reached home after driving aimlessly through the countryside for almost an hour her father was waiting for her, standing out on the porch, clutching a book.

"Lord, Suzannah, where have you been? I was getting quite anxious."

"Sorry." She ran lightly up the steps and kissed him. "I ran into someone I knew." He followed her into the kitchen where she immediately put the kettle on for a cup of tea. *Tea.* She suspected everyone resorted to it in shock.

"Sit down, Father. I have something to tell you."

He took a long look at her. "I hope it's good," he mumbled, pulling out a chair and settling into it.

"I know you won't think so." She took down two cups and saucers, placed them on the table. "The company that bought Bellemont..."

"Yes?" he enquired gruffly.

"Is a front for Nick Konrads." She went to him and placed her hands on his shoulders. "Please don't upset yourself more than you have to. But you have to know."

She was unprepared for his reaction. Her father bowed his head so low his forehead almost touched the table. "God, haven't I dreaded this day," he groaned.

"You knew it would happen?"

He nodded. "I've never met anyone like Konrads in my life. In a way I suppose I've been afraid of him. Does that sound silly to you?"

"No." She understood her father's reaction perfectly.

"Why didn't we *know?*" he said, his right hand jerking with nerves.

"I suppose we felt Nick would never want to come back to this town again."

Her father shifted uncomfortably, drumming his fingers against the rich timber of the table. "He's the cool one, isn't he?"

"He's a very rich man these days." She crossed to the counter and spooned tea into the china pot.

"I have been following his career," her father said

dryly, taking a cigar out of his breast pocket and lighting it, though she turned away from the blue puff of smoke.

"You shouldn't be doing that," she warned him, opening the window. "The doctor has told you. I hate to see you doing damage to your lungs."

"What does it matter now?" he answered, his voice harsh with what she now recognised as self-pity. "So, is he still in love with you?" He looked up and fixed her with the intensity of his gaze. "You saw him, didn't you. You went up to the house?"

She let out her breath slowly. "Nick was the last person I ever expected to see." She poured boiling water into the teapot, determined to take hers outside. Her father had really tried to give up smoking, now stress was eating away at him.

"Which doesn't answer my question," he replied.

"Nick hates us, Father." She turned on him, her voice as hard as his. "Would you expect anything else?"

"God Almighty. I could have had him in jail. Doesn't he realise how lucky he was?"

Was she always to be confronted by his lies? "Father, when are you going to admit to yourself I *know?*"

He frowned, bracing his hands against the table. "Know *what?*" With no outlets for his frustration he was beginning to confront Suzannah and Charlotte with it.

"The plan you hatched up years ago for Martin to carry out." Suzannah didn't back off.

Absolute silence from her father. She spoke again. "I tell you, I *know*. Martin finally had to confess."

"Of course he would!" Her father barked with contempt, his speech slurring a little as it did when he became agitated. "Why didn't I know he was too weak to come into our family?"

"How would you do it if you had to do it all over

again?'' Quietly Suzannah put his tea in front of him, feeling sick.

"Exactly the same!'' His tall body stiffened, his expression more irascible than ever. "The last thing in the world I wanted was for you to marry that boy. It was a mistake to have ever encouraged him. Had him near the house. Too sure of himself by far. Always so damned arrogant. Always summing you up with those black eyes.''

"He took great care of me.''

Even her father had to acknowledge it. He shook his head at the same time stabbing out his cigar on the saucer. "I looked on him kindly enough until you both began to grow up. Then I saw him for what he was.''

"Please tell me?'' she begged. "What was he?''

"The man who would take you away from me forever.'' Her father bowed his head.

# CHAPTER FOUR

HE ROAMED the estate for most of the day, filled with a bittersweet nostalgia that had Suzannah at the centre. Remembrance of things past. Playing here together twenty-odd years ago. The banks upon banks of azaleas and rhododendrons he had always loved greeted him everywhere in exquisite profusion, some of the rhododendrons as tall as trees, filling the green landscape with a wealth of colour, the range of pinks, the rich reds, the purples, the snowy-white drifts, the gorgeous golden yellow and orange. As he approached the stables complex he became a little morbid. The stables were now deserted, the horses all sold off, those splendid creatures that had offered him so much peace and pleasure.

Under a brilliant blue sky he walked the formal acres of vines that covered the steeper stony slopes in a quivering sea of delicate green and gold. Vitus Vinifera. The sacred wine, its cultivation lost in the mists of antiquity. Down amid the regimented aisles of vines, he carefully examined the Rhine rieslings with their distinctive spring shoots coloured red. The three-lobed leaves were rough and puckered on top, the spotted yellowy green berries sitting in small tight cylindrical bunches. He cradled them gently, breathing in the incomparable scent of earth and plant. Public taste for many years had favoured the Chardonnays as the premium white table wine but he had always favoured the famous grape of the Rhine Valley, preferring their fresh distinctive fruitiness and flavour to the more delicate character of the Chardonnay. All this

was his responsibility now. He'd had no idea the vineyards had been so neglected. There were signs of dete-
rioration everywhere. The harvest would be of poorer
quantity and quality. That would stop. Big plans began
circulating in his mind. Hans Schroeder and his son, Kurt,
would have to be brought back. The Schroeder family,
German in origin like German settlers who had established so many famous wineries of the Barossa Valley in
South Australia, were devoted to winemaking, with a fine
record of achievement. They had worked for the Sheffield
family vineyard since the winery had been established in
the early 1800s when Edward Sheffield, the then master
of Bellemont and a man apparently of tremendous vision,
had decided to produce noteworthy wines for his own
table and tables of his pastoralist friends.

The old two-storey stone winery with its underground
tunnels was a wonderfully picturesque old place impreg-
nated with the aroma of wine, the soft amber brick of the
facade decorated with a beautiful violet flowering trum-
pet vine. Like Suzannah's eyes. The winery would have
to be better equipped, thoroughly modernised. He had
very little free time but he would set the right people to
work on upgrading and expansion. Many more acres
could go under the vine. Semillon, Chardonnay. They
would stick to the white styles, concentrating on quality
and refinement. He would have to bring in a vineyard
director and perhaps one of the new young vignerons
doing such great things. It would create work for people
of the district. Nick realised now it would be a thrilling
challenge to make top-quality table wines. Concentrating
on the vineyards he would turn the stables into a teaching
establishment, offering riding lessons to all the children
of the district, not just the rich kids, all the kids with his
same love of horses. Maybe keep better horses for the

use of accomplished adult riders. It should be easy
enough to find the right person to run the place.

Inevitably he thought of Suzannah. She was an exceptional horsewoman with a natural affinity for those most
beautiful and delicate long-legged creatures. He thought
of the times they had ridden together, galloping everywhere; over the hills, walking their horses beside the
river, revelling in the communication between each other
and the splendid mounts Suzannah selected for their
rides. It was always a source of amazement to him that
her father hadn't objected to his riding any of the quality
horses but then Marcus Sheffield, for all his arrogance
and snobbish ways, knew full well how he could ride and
how much he cared about horses. He had to thank
Suzannah for his riding lessons as well. She had insisted
he share so many of her training sessions after her coach
immediately realised he had an affinity with these extraordinary animals. He could, in fact, sit on anything
from a rogue to a thoroughbred almost from the beginning.

He walked back through the lemon grove, breathing in
the wonderful citrus aroma. Here he was a migrant kid
of no importance, master of Bellemont. But that was
Australia. Anyone with the brains and the ambition could
make it to the very top.

Towards afternoon he drove into the town, parking the
Mercedes in the side street alongside the town's primary
school. Many more cars were beginning to pull in on the
main street as mothers arrived to collect their children.
No sign of the Sheffield Rolls Suzannah had been driving
yesterday. Maybe she had a car of her own. One he
wouldn't recognise.

He almost missed her in the crowd. Children began to

pour out of their classrooms, running headlong across the beautiful tree-shaded playground and out the front and side gates into their mothers' arms. These were the little ones. Grade One and Two. The older children would be let out later. Sitting deep in his seat he straightened, staring out the window. The children were all wearing hats, protection against the sun. The uniforms of the little girls were all the same. It would be near impossible to spot Charlotte, the mirror image of her mother, among that lot. He had to keep his eye strained for Suzannah's appearance. He would know her even bundled up in a raincoat with the hood pulled down over her eyes. No one moved with her grace. No one had her elegant legs even in jeans.

At the last moment he spotted her. She was moving very quickly, clutching the hand of a little girl, throwing many quick looks around her.

"Damn you, Suzannah," he thought. She was very, very anxious to prevent him from seeing her daughter.

*Why?*

He had to swallow on a hard knot in his chest to regain his composure. He knew how old the child was. He knew her name. He knew Suzannah had betrayed him only to marry Martin White an unaccountably short time later.

She wasn't going to get away. He opened the door of the Mercedes unaware of the acute attention that was now being given to him. All conversation stopped. Heads turned.

He grabbed Suzannah's hand just as she opened the passenger door of her small white hatchback, inconspicuous among so many others, speaking pleasantly so as not to alarm the child.

"Suzannah. How marvellous to see you again." He

smiled as he said it, the smile wonderfully softening his arresting features.

"Nick." She was very pale, only one step away from throwing the child in the car.

"Good afternoon." Now he transferred his smile to the little girl who was staring up at him with huge, almond-set blue-green eyes. Changeable eyes. Like the sea. Eyes that could look very blue or green according to the colours she wore. The shock stopped his heart. These lovely eyes held a peculiar expression, pleasure mingled with a puzzled recognition. Her apple blossom skin was flushed, her thick dark hair emerged from her school hat in a long plait tied at the end with a ribbon.

"I was just passing when I saw you," he tried his hardest to speak normally when he felt like keening his pain to the heavens. "Won't you introduce me to your beautiful daughter?"

"Hi!" Charlotte piped up before her mother could manage a word. Like a little lady she gave him her hand. "I'm Charley. It's really Charlotte but everyone calls me Charley."

"Delighted to meet you, Charley." Desperately he held back his roaring primal emotions. He looked down at the milky baby-soft skin of the hand enclosed in his. Charlotte. My daughter. My God! He sensed it as an animal senses its young.

"And how are you?" Charley smiled up at him happily thinking how wonderfully handsome he was, his eyes so brilliant—sort of like black diamonds. Where had she seen him before? She would think of it in a minute.

"My name is Nicholas Konrads, Charlotte." In his monstrous confusion, heart hammering in his chest, he used her full name. "I used to be good friends with your mother."

"Were you? How wonderful. Ah, now I know!" The little girl looked from him to her mother. "I found a lot of pictures of you and mummy once." Full recognition danced in her eyes. "Mummy had forgotten all about them. They were in an album. It was hidden away in a cupboard. Mummy said you were cousins. Are you my cousin, too?"

"Honorary cousin, darling," Suzannah intervened tautly. "That's what I mean. Mr Konrads is no relation."

Like hell I'm not, he thought violently. Anger pounded in him, wanting to shake Suzannah until her bones rattled.

"Look, it's lovely to see you, Nick, but we've got to run. Hectic scarlet stained Suzannah's magnolia cheeks.

"Perhaps I might visit you," he managed to say almost levelly, looking her very piercingly in the eyes.

"How about coffee tomorrow," she suggested in a moment of pure panic. She didn't think for a moment Nick would just go away.

"I won't be here tomorrow," he said, still overwhelmed by the sight of this small girl. "I have to be back in Sydney. What about tonight? Could you manage dinner? A restaurant, of course." He could see the helpless fluttering of a pulse in her throat. Felt a vivid anger mixed up with grief.

She feigned a rueful smile, determined on headlong flight. "No good tonight, Nick. I really have to be at home for Charley." "No, you don't, Mamma," Charlotte said, pulling on her mother's arm. Although she wasn't participating in the conversation she was very involved. "Grandpa can look after me." Charlotte was deeply worried about her mother, aware of her hidden sorrows. It would be very nice for mummy to have dinner with Mr Konrads. Charlotte could see straight off he was a very special person. She remembered the lots of photographs

from when Mummy was quite small, always with the
same tall boy at her shoulder. Then years later Mummy
as a teenager astride a big horse, back so straight, helping
with the harvest, playing the piano, curled up on a sofa,
dressed for dances. Mr Konrads was in most of them. He
still looked the same except for the shorter hair and the
grown-up clothes and kind of *importance* Grandpa used
to have before he became ill.

"I know where your house is, Suzannah," he said,
looking at her over the child's head, his eyes conveying
all the things he couldn't say. It was all out of her control
now.

Suzannah for her part was receiving the full impact of
his reaction. She felt physically ill, her legs rubbery.
Charley was looking up into his face, head cocked to one
side, a smile on her rosebud mouth. It was very obvious
she has taken to him on sight. Why not? My God why
not? Inside her heart broke.

"Do you know where the Chantilly Cafe used to be?"
she asked, feeling the full force of his powerful personality.

"Of course." He cursed himself when the words came
out clipped.

"There's a very good restaurant there now," Suzannah
said almost frantically, "Augustine's. I'll met you there.
It won't be until around eight, I'm afraid."

"Can't Mr Konrads pick you up?" Charley whispered,
because she didn't like her mother driving alone at night.
It wasn't safe. Like Daddy. She had to know her mother
would be safe.

"You're making Charlotte anxious," he found himself
pointing out, effortlessly reading the message in those
blue-green eyes. "I'll be outside your house at eight

o'clock exactly. I won't disturb your father.'' If I did I might pound him. Sickness or not.

"You won't really disturb us,'' Charley said in her child's lilt, hoping to get the opportunity to see Mummy's friend again.

She was too sweet not to do anything else. On impulse he went down on his haunches, some expression in his eyes causing the little girl to suddenly fling herself forward, burying her face in the hollow of his neck. He couldn't stand it. He forgot he was supposed to be a complete stranger to her and put his arms around her, stroking her back.

"Oh, Nick!'' Suzannah's small cry was that of a wounded bird's, spiralling up.

"Promise I'll see you again.'' Charley said, pushing her hat right back off her head.

He straightened to his full height, laying his hand on the silky crown of her head, bound to her as surely as he was bound to her mother. "Charlotte, I promise you'll see me for the rest of my life.''

It was a promise all three of them were to remember.

There was no way she could lie to her father. Besides, Charley was full of the meeting outside the school, chatting away happily until her grandfather stopped her with a ferocious look.

"That will do, Charley,'' he said sternly, causing the little girl to blush.

"I'm sorry, Grandpa.

"Why don't you run up and get changed, precious.'' Suzannah got a tight hold on her own anger. Feeling the way she did about her daughter she wasn't going to subject her to her father's increasingly testy moods. It was the futility of his life that was getting to him, the severe reversal in their fortunes. Now Nick had returned to teach them both a lesson.

"Yes, Mamma." Charley looked over to her mother who smiled at her encouragingly.

"I'll have some nice afternoon tea ready for you when you get back."

"Maybe I'm not hearing this properly?" her father began as soon as Charlotte disappeared. "Nick Konrads came to the school?"

"He was passing. That's all." Suzannah took milk from the fridge intending to add some chocolate Milo.

Her father shuffled to a chair and shook his head. "Don't give me that. He's seeking you out. He'd better look out I don't catch sight of him."

Suzannah shrugged, thinking her father's days of ascendancy were all over. "I'm having dinner with him tonight."

That almost deprived her father of breath. "You're what?" His cheeks flushed. "This man is a thief!"

"I thought we'd settled all that, Father," she said as quietly as she could. "Please don't raise your voice. I don't want Charley upset."

"No, but you want to upset me." Marcus Sheffield's tone was harsh and ugly. "I forbid you to go out of this house tonight, Suzannah. You have a child to look after, if not me."

"Father, please, don't ruin everything for us," she begged, feeling at the end of her tether. "I don't want to argue with you. I'm a grown woman. I'm hardly away from you and Charley for a minute. Nick is too powerful to ignore. He wants to speak to me."

"About what?" Marcus Sheffield sounded outraged. "Don't tell *me* he's a dangerous man. I know that. I wish he'd gone back to the country where he was born."

"We all came from somewhere, Father," she countered wearily. "Only the aborigines inhabited this land."

Her father ignored her. "It doesn't matter to you I'm utterly against your seeing him."

"It doesn't matter at all," she was driven to admit. "Not this time around. I loved Nick, Father. I loved him with all my heart. I knew he was going to ask me to marry him. I was going to say yes. We were made for each other. Pure and simple. But you and Martin destroyed all that."

"Why oh why did I lose all my money?" Her father moaned, unwilling or unable to respond to her charge. "Why oh why did I put so much trust in Martin?"

"I told you. He was one of *us*. One of the privileged."

"And yet I regret nothing." Marcus Sheffield's faded eyes flashed.

"That's the pity of it, Father," Suzannah said.

There were more words a half an hour before Nick was due to arrive and Suzannah, sunk in near despair, decided she couldn't possibly leave Charley with her father. To a certain extent he had changed into another person, leaving the child both wary and bewildered. She would have to run out to the car and explain as much as she dared to Nick. She rarely left her father to take care of Charlotte, always taking his diminished health into consideration, but never had his flaring temper been so much in evidence.

He had never been so unhappy in his life. He has never really lost control of me, Suzannah thought. Indulgent to a fault, her father in some ways had been the worst kind of father. Perhaps even now his behaviour was meant to control her. There was no way she could meet Nick if she left an anxious little daughter at home.

*No way.*

"There aren't many fathers who've been as generous and supportive as I," he told her icily, even with Charley hovering uncertainly in the background. "I had you and Martin live with me. I've as good as reared your child. You all came to me for money."

"You taught us all to be dependant, Father," Suzannah countered. "That's the way you wanted it." She went to Charley and turned her about. "Bedtime, my darling. School tomorrow."

"Are you still going out?" Charley asked, thinking Grandpa was being horrible to Mummy.

"No, darling," Suzannah answered in a calm, reassuring voice. "Grandpa isn't well. It's not the time to leave you."

A surge of new life seemed to burst on Marcus Sheffield. "I'm glad you had the sense to see that," he called. "You're still a dreamer, Suzannah. Hankering after things that are bad for you."

"Why does Grandpa hate Mr Konrads so much?" In her small bedroom highly intelligent little Charley fixed her mother with a straight look.

"He doesn't hate him, darling." Suzannah tucked her daughter in, bending to kiss Charley lightly as the little girl puckered her lips.

"He sure doesn't love him," Charley said with almost adult irony. "I think it's awful Grandpa won't let you go out tonight."

Children saw very clearly. "I decided that myself, pet. Looking after children is beyond Grandpa these days."

"But I'll be in bed *asleep*," Charley reasoned. She really wanted her mother to see Mr. Konrads again. Her mother was so sad and Mr. Konrads had been such a good friend.

"Go to sleep now, darling," Suzannah soothed. "You're quite safe. I'm staying home."

"Safe and warm." Charley yawned. "I don't know why Daddy didn't love me."

For a moment Suzannah was overwhelmed by anguish. "He *did*, Charley. You must remember not everyone is a very affectionate person. They don't show it with lots of hugs and kisses."

"Like you," Charley said gratefully, turning on her side and positioning her hands under her cheek. "Mr. Konrads put his arms around me. He hugged me and stroked my back. I was really happy when he did that. It was like I'd known him for a long, long time. Isn't that funny?" For a moment Suzannah was overwhelmed by anguish.

"You're a mighty pretty little rose. Pleasant dreams, my love."

"Night, night, Mummy," Charley said, her eyelids already falling to lie like silky black wings on her velvet cheeks.

"What do you propose to do about Konrads?" her father asked later with a return to his old arrogant demeanour. "Let me handle it."

Suzannah kept her voice under control. "I've suffered a lot because of the way you handled things, Father. I'm going out to explain to Nick the change of plan. You'd be well advised to keep out of it."

He read her determination in the tilt of her chin. "I'm very disappointed in you, Suzannah. You're getting very hard."

Why wasn't I years ago, she thought, but held her tongue.

She waited out on the porch, running down the pathway to the gate as soon as she caught sight of the

Mercedes coming down the street. She had dressed quietly for the evening, playing down her looks, not knowing the reverse was true. The midnight-blue of her camisole, matching pants and jacket deepened the beauty of
her eyes and the creamy clarity of her skin. Her hair
pulled back and tucked behind her ears showed off the
shape of her face, the small shell-like setting of her ears,
the line of her chin and neck. Her beauty, a special gift,
had never brought her any happiness. It had brought her
trouble.

As Nick parked the car she opened up the passenger
door and slid in as though she could scarcely wait to be
away. Dark fire burned in him. He switched on the interior light, the better to see her, immediately aware of
the anxiety that was brimming in her.

"What's the matter?" He almost reached out to pull
her thick glossy hair loose then decided this way he had
a better view of her high-cheekboned face.

"Nick, I can't go with you." Her voice shook a little,
her body trembled, all borne of his powerful effect on
her and fear of what her father might do.

"Can't or won't?" He sounded languid, the sardonic
tone of his voice exaggerated.

"Father simply isn't well enough to leave," she said
in a low voice.

He gave a mirthless laugh. "I should believe it but
somehow it doesn't sound right to me. Your father is the
most manipulative, controlling old devil in the world. It's
*bad,* Suzannah, and you shouldn't put up with it. Why
the hell didn't you and poor gutless Martin fly the coop?
Didn't you want to be on your own?"

The stark truth overrode her. "No, I *didn't*," she found
herself saying. God forgive her she didn't love Martin
but she had the magic of Bellemont. She had the horses
whose presence gave her enormous comfort. She had her

daily walks through the vineyard. Her beloved little daughter revelled in her environment, loving it as much as her mother. She didn't go. She couldn't go. Martin, too, had been very mindful of all the benefits. His job for which her father paid him generously, a splendid colonial mansion—one of the best in the land—to call home.

"Whatever happened to all that wonderful proud spirit? Suzannah my little firebrand," Nick mocked.

"Nick, I must go," she said desperately, her feelings for him flowing as deep as ever.

He reached out and encircled her wrist, finding it too fragile. "Why are you under such terrible strain?" he demanded.

"Why do you think?" she replied emotionally. "I lost my husband not so long ago. He was killed in a car crash. He had another woman with him at the time. I've lost my home. Not any old home but the place where my family has lived forever. My father has had a stroke. He's lost his money. And you ask why am I stressed?"

"Stressed as in tonight," he rasped. "I know all the rest."

"Father still hates you, Nick," she said in a stricken voice.

His dark face tautened. "Which leaves me utterly cold. Deep in your heart you know the reason for it all. Your mother left him. Ran away. You're never going to be allowed to do that."

It was dreadfully close to the truth. "You forget he could have another stroke at any time. I don't want that on my head."

"Oh, Suzannah, don't carry the guilt. Your father has lived the good life to the hilt. I remember he was furious when his doctor told him he had to quit smoking and limit his intake of alcohol. You weren't party to any of that but you are party to a massive deception.'' He kept his brilliant eyes on her.

"I don't know what you're talking about.'' She tried ineffectually to free her hand.

"Ah, but you do,'' he said in a voice that was perfectly hard. "If I weren't a civilised man I might close my hands around your throat.''

She shivered, her heart beating a tattoo. "I never thought you had violence in you.''

"Neither did I,'' he responded, "until I saw my daughter's face.''

Wanting more than anything to escape his condemnation, Suzannah released her hand, jerking backwards, giving a bitter, incredulous laugh. "Is that why you wanted to see me? You thought Charley was your daughter?''

"I *know* Charlotte is my daughter,'' he said in a terrifying voice. "She has my mother's name. She has my mother's eyes. Those wonderful changeable blue-green. The *exact* shape. God, Suzannah, did no one else see it?''

Fear leapt in her. "You must have forgotten Martin's sister. Sheridan has those colour eyes.''

His hand tightened as he looked at her. "I'm talking about *extraordinary* eyes, Suzannah. Eyes that run in families. I remember both of Martin's sisters well. Neither of them had eyes that dominated the face. Yours are a wonderful violet. Charley inherited all the rest from you—the triangular face, the hair, the light, long limbs— but she got my *mother's* eyes. You can't walk away from that.''

"But I'm going to.'' She shook her head vehemently so the full weight of her hair on one side slid forward.

"You've got things badly wrong. Charley is Martin's daughter."

"You can lie even now," he said coldly, a powerful anger stirring.

"Do you want a child so badly you would take mine?" She stared at him, her eyes trapped.

"And *mine*. Don't play me for a fool. I have many, many, contacts in the medical and scientific world. Charlotte threw herself into my arms…why, Suzannah? Have you asked yourself that? She left a long strand of her hair on my jacket. I've packed it away in an envelope. You know all about DNA testing. It's in all the news. All I need is one strand of Charlotte's hair to claim her as my child."

"You're mad." Her voice broke.

"You're the mad one if you keep playing this stupid charade," he told her harshly. "Why did you do it? Why did you wrong me? You've kept my beautiful child hidden from me all these years. Do you know what incredible pain I feel? I missed her birth. I missed her infancy. I missed all the wonderful years when she turned from a toddler into the little girl she is now. I've been alone, Suzannah. *Alone.*"

"Alone?" She fairly crackled with nerves. "Every time I saw you in a magazine or a newspaper you were with some woman. You've built up a huge business. You're a multimillionaire. You can afford to buy Bellemont."

"I slaved to get it," he said, his own eyes blazing. "It came at a high cost."

She looked away. "Charley isn't your daughter, Nick."

"What an actress you are!" He smiled lightly. "Who are you trying to protect, Suzannah? Yourself? You've acted with dishonour. Martin must have been dreadfully unhappy knowing Charlotte was never his.''

Her voice was loud and brittle in the quiet leather-scented interior of the car. ''Never in our whole married life did he accuse me of such a thing.''

''It was all too painful, I suppose,'' Nick retorted. ''And what of your father? God alone knows how he kept his suspicions to himself.''

''Don't.'' She stared at him, her eyes like jewels in her pale face. ''Charley is *my* daughter. She's the image of me. Father adores her.''

''She is, after all, your child.'' He nodded, sounding reasonable.

It gave her hope. ''Nick, I must go back inside the house. We have to put an end to this conversation.''

''You don't want to leave Charlotte in your father's care?'' he asked with sharp intuition.

''It's just that he's not up to it.''

''Odd when she's most probably asleep.'' He looked towards the lights of the house. ''Why don't I simply drive off?''

''Please don't, Nick.'' She showed her vulnerability, letting her fingers clutch his arm.

''I suppose you've spent all day arguing with him,'' he said in a pained voice. ''I know better than anyone how much power he has over you. Why don't you get a house of your own? Did Martin have nothing to leave you?'' he added with disgust.

''Martin made too many mistakes.'' She was simply beyond explaining.

''Not the least of them marrying you,'' he said curtly. ''Is that why he spent time with other women? He couldn't bear the pain of knowing you didn't love him.''

Tears sprang to her eyes. "No one has the right to speak to me like that," she told him passionately.

"I believe *I* have," he said gratingly, going with the turbulent current that flowed between them. Rejection, humiliation, loss, rose like bile in the back of his throat.

"Why is it men love power?" she asked. "Power above any woman. This is a contest between you and my father."

He turned his shoulders to stare at her lovely patrician face. "Believe that and you'll believe anything. I admit it started that way. Started me on the road to success. I needed money, big money to make those who had wronged me suffer. But revenge is like acid. It eats into the soul. Any revenge I've had is empty. Too much has happened. Your father may *think* he is, but he's no longer a player. He can't move us all around like pawns on a board. Martin is gone. Poor, unhappy Martin doomed to love you. Your life has been blighted to guilt and lies. And me? I've been cut to the heart by the sight of my own child."

It was terrible to hear him say it. She felt hounded, pressed to the wall. "I told you, *no.*" Her voice was filled with an overwhelming rage of emotion. She didn't need all this pain. This grieving. Now this charge she *couldn't* hear. Pinned to the passenger seat she felt as if she was sliding precariously across ice, careering towards a deep black hole.

"You never used to be a liar." He caught the point of her chin, his fingers strong and hurting. "We'll get to the truth, Suzannah. Then God help you."

"I told you. Let me go, Nick," she snapped. "My whole life is upsetting and difficult. I don't need this extra trauma. We were only together once." *Once!* When the memory of those passionate, tempestuous shared hours had stayed with her every day of her life. Even when Martin was making love to her she was terrified she would call out Nick's name.

"Once is all it takes," he pointed out bluntly, moving his palm over the curve of her cheek, down the slope of her jawline to her slender, vulnerable throat. He had a feeling of being on the extreme edge yet she stared back at him, her beautiful violet eyes stark, clear…brave.

"I want you." It was torn from him. He never wanted to *say* it. "I can't recall a minute I haven't wanted you since I knew what sexual desire was all about."

"So you took other women instead?" she said, unable to control her own bitterness.

"With *passing* pleasure, Suzannah. Never a consuming need." His thumb traced the line of her jaw. "How can love exist alongside hate?" he asked, too gently.

"You *hate* me?" She held his wrist, contrition pouring from her.

"What you've done cries out for hatred. The pity of it all!" he groaned. The pain, the anger, the disillusionment. "You were everything in the world to me yet you shoved me aside for Martin White. God pity him."

"I loved Martin," she said, refusing to admit the naked truth.

"You loved money, position, your status in the district," he corrected her starkly. "You loved *Bellemont*. You wanted that more than anything else. Your father might have disinherited you had you run off with me." Her near-black hair brushed his hand, thick, satiny, scented.

"Nothing to be gained by looking back at the past," she said sadly, the soft glow of the interior light painting her skin with delicate apricot.

"The past is always with us, Suzannah." He tried to

force his brain into giving the command to his hand to let go of her but she was every desire imaginable mixed into one. Hunger was an expanding force in his chest. It pounded against his rib cage like a wild animal desperate to get out.

The soft, low camisole she wore beneath her open jacket showed the swell of her breasts, like creamy roses. He saw now she wasn't wearing a bra and he felt like plunging his hand into her mauve shadowed cleavage, voluptuously cupping her breasts, teasing the puckered berries of her nipples. The world was spinning away on a sizzling burn of desire....

Suzannah naked beside him, her beautiful limbs silvered by moonlight. Outside the rustle of leaves as the night wind played gently through the graceful branches of gum trees, the patches of sky they could see through the open French doors filled with the glittering diamonds of stars. The scent of her as they lay there, both of them so extravagantly fulfilled and happy it was like a vision of Heaven. She did not refuse him. She loved him. She had loved him as a child. She loved him as a man. This was the first time for both of them. A momentous threshold passed. This was life itself.

*Life.*

He had planted his seed in that glorious ritual of love.

In a blur, not trying to stop it, his black eyes brilliant, he pressed on her sensitive nape until her face was where he wanted it, a scant inch from his own. In a way it fulfilled some of his bittersweet fantasies. He kissed her then, making no bones about his hunger nor his profound sense of possession. She was the gorgeous butterfly on the end of a pin. She was his.

## CHAPTER FIVE

IT DIDN'T take him long to get the results of the DNA
testing. In a way it had been an imperative irrefutable
proof but he had known in his bones and his blood and
his heart that Charlotte was his child. That enchanting
little girl with her mother's heart-shaped face and her
grandmother's iridescent eyes was the result of that one
night he and Suzannah had surrendered to a passion that
had grown too big for them both. It broke his heart now
to think Suzannah had allowed Martin White to take his
place, to raise *his* daughter as Martin's own.

Suzannah had a great deal to answer for. With the results of the testing on his desk he felt certain he couldn't
forgive her. Six years of Charlotte's young life had gone.
Six years he had missed. Six years he would yearn for
for the rest of his life. He had left Ashbury telling
Suzannah he would return once he had the proof he
needed. Proof of paternity. Armed with this knowledge
there were going to be big changes in all of their lives.
This time he knew he wouldn't lose the battle.

When Adrienne all but barged into his office, smiling
as she did so, Bebe behind her looking flushed, a little
frantic with apology, he was holding the document in his
hands. He let it fall, covering it partially with other papers. As Bebe conveyed with her mobile face, Adrienne
had simply pushed her way in.

"Thank you, Bebe," he smiled to reassure her.

"I need to see you, Nick." Adrienne's voice had a

cajoling pitch to it. "I'm sure Bebe guards you better than the secret service do the president."

"That's my job," Bebe said. Nothing could make her take to Nick's current lady friend. She was very glamorous, of course. Very sleek in her narrow tailored suit, her short chestnut hair like little licks of flame around her strongly modelled face, but Bebe found her a lot less than engaging. She was all over Nick, which might have had something to do with it, but Adrienne Alleman had little time to spare for her own sex or anyone who hadn't *arrived* in this world, Bebe thought.

As she retreated Adrienne came around Nick's desk and dropped a kiss on the high ridge of his cheek. "You haven't rung me for a week," she said, pouting.

"I've been terribly busy, Adrienne," he explained casually. "A program for Grantley Stables merchant bank." Grantley, a friend of his, had taken over from his late father and was determined on making sweeping changes.

"I know how it is!" Adrienne sighed. "You work much too hard." She touched a hand to his raven hair. "Can't we possibly have lunch?"

She leaned down and put her hand over his, thrilling to the sensation of skin on skin. Nick Konrads was the sexiest, the most exciting man she had ever known. And she had known quite a few. She was avid for him. For his time.

"Why not?" It would have been callous to say no. Callous not to wind her down gently. Give her an indication what he proposed to do with his life. He knew damned well it would hurt her. He was feeling sorry in advance, but he had been very careful not to make Adrienne any promises. They were friends. She knew he saw other women from time to time.

But never now. The flame that had burned so long, so blindly for Suzannah Sheffield endured, even though it scorched him with its heat.

"Wonderful!" Her face lit up with delighted relief. "I'm so pleased I came in now even if your Bebe was trying to chase me away," she added archly.

"Not at all." He stood up. "Bebe knows my workload better than anyone. I rely on her so much."

"I'm sure, darling," Adrienne said, glad beyond words Bebe Marshall was a plumb middle-aged frump.

"Speaking of which, there are a few things I must tell her," Nick remembered. "Take a seat for a moment, Adrienne. I won't be long."

Adrienne watched him walk out of his office in search of his secretary. How marvellous he looked in his clothes, so tall, broad shouldered, torso tapering to a trim waist and lean hips. How elegantly he dressed. She loved his expensive suits, the fine shirts, silk ties. The body of an athlete, a natural clothes horse. And without them! A miracle of male power and grace. Just thinking about him naked brought her out in a high heat.

As she went to move around the desk, her eyes quite inadvertently fell on some papers on his desk.

How extraordinary! She drew a deep breath, leaning forward swiftly, deliberately, to study a document tucked under a sheaf of papers. She recognised the name of the laboratory, saw the stamp Private & Confidential. It was about DNA testing, not unusual given Nick's business and the institutions he devised programs for, but she was certain they wouldn't be stamped that way. In some deep intuitive way she knew this piece of paper meant trouble. Once started she couldn't stop. She read through the document from start to finish, cold fear springing up like tendrils getting a grip on her heart. She couldn't lose

Nick. Not now. That would be unbearable. She would never find anyone else remotely like him. So handsome, so brilliant, so *rich*. No one could hold a candle to Nick. Yet Nick Konrads had a child.

Adrienne guessed without an instant's hesitation who the mother might be.

Nick as good as confirmed it over lunch. Though it angered her greatly, Adrienne gave him the lead to reveal what was going on in his life. If Nick was going to turn his back on her, someone was going to be made to suffer.

"It's wonderful what we have together," she told him, looking through her heavy lashes. "We enjoy each other's company. You're a glorious lover but somehow I've always had the feeling you won't trust me with your deepest confidence." She kept her voice low, rich, sympathetic. "There was *someone* you didn't marry, Nick. Someone who hurt you dreadfully. Is it so hard for you to tell me?"

He smiled that magical smile everyone waited for. "We all have our little secrets, Adrienne. Things we keep locked away." Just faintly he lifted his chiselled chin. A warning perhaps to keep off?

In an excess of jealousy, Adrienne decided to carry on. "That woman you were speaking to at the funeral. It was her husband, wasn't it?"

"Come on, Adrienne," he said. "I thought we'd been over that."

"You were in love with her, weren't you? Don't freeze me out, Nick. I promise you, I'm only trying to help."

"I don't know that I need your help, Adrienne," he said mildly, lifting his wineglass to his mouth.

"Everyone needs help," she assured him in a caring voice. "I would miss you dreadfully, Nick, if you went out of my life but somehow I think that is about to happen."

He felt deeply for her then. "I hope not. Isn't it possible for us to remain friends? There has never been any talk of marriage between us, Adrienne."

She made a small sound of regret. "I know that. But doesn't it strike you the longer we're together how right it seems?"

The moment couldn't be put off any longer. He leaned forward, taking her hand. "Adrienne, I never did mean to lead you on or waste your time. I enjoy your companionship. It's meant a lot."

She couldn't help making a harsh, exasperated sound. "It was simply the sex, wasn't it, Nick?" Her jealous face said it all.

He shook his head emphatically. "More than that, Adrienne. There's no need to put yourself down. You're an attractive, intelligent experienced woman. You're worldly enough to take our affair in your stride."

"Which presupposes I have no intention of remarrying?" she retorted, feeling an urgent desire to scream.

"I imagine you will. You have a lot to offer the right man. I'm so sorry if it hurts you, but I'm not that man, Adrienne."

"Because you're in love with someone else?" she said emotionally. It was something she would have to deal with. "That young woman. She's the barrier." She'd damn well check her out.

"It was a terribly sad funeral, wasn't it." He looked away, a sombre expression on his striking face. "Sad to see a man die long before his prime."

"How come you didn't marry her?" Adrienne wanted to return to her theme. "It's obvious to me now she's the one you wanted."

"Do you really want to know?" His black gaze was ironic.

"Try me?"

"It's something I never talk about, Adrienne," he said shaking his head. "It was a profoundly unhappy time in life."

"So why did you go back?" She wasn't exactly sure she understood.

"Because, my dear, it's not over yet."

Wasn't that as good as an admission? Adrienne thought. What she really needed was inside information and that could be gained for a price.

For days Suzannah agonised over telling her father the truth: Charley was Nick's child. She had known that all along. Before her pregnancy had been confirmed. That one time they had been together was simply too glorious, too full of the fever and intensity that produced life. Her father's and Martin's actions had cost them all dearly. She had thought to get help from Charlotte Konrads, a woman already seared by grief and the added torment of what had happened to her son. She should have told Charlotte of the sickness that wasn't going away. It seemed preposterous to her now but without a mother, no serene female relative to turn to, what was happening to her came as a kind of terror. That was Nick's baby growing inside of her and Nick had gone away. Never abusing her but grim and silent, refusing to meet her. There was no way, it seemed, that Charlotte Konrads had considered the young woman she had known from childhood was now pregnant to her son. Suzannah Sheffield had brought him enough trouble. Charlotte would not think of ever trusting her again. Suzannah, in her way, had been rejected.

So she married Martin. Indeed her father had propelled her into it so swiftly it was as though their lives depended on it. There was no way he could have known she was pregnant. She didn't tell a soul. She hadn't in fact even "shown" until her seventh month. By then Martin and her father had settled happily into waiting for the arrival of the Sheffield-White heir. Her father had adored Charley from the moment she was put into his arms. Martin, very strangely, believing this perfect little girl to be his own had made no real connection with her in the deep nurturing way one would expect of a loving father. During her whole childhood he rarely played with Charley, seemingly unable to reach out to her or show his affection. Not that he was ever unkind or reprimanded her harshly. That in any case would never have been tolerated with Suzannah and Marcus Sheffield obviously doting on this sweet and beautiful child. It was as though Martin knew in his heart the child his wife lived for wasn't his. Just as he knew his suspicion was unspeakable. His own family lavished love on Charley, welcoming her visits. Far too many reasons for the truth ever to be known.

Then as now.

The shock of finding out might precipitate another stroke, Suzannah thought in agony now. There seemed no way she could share her burden. There was even a possibility her father might turn on Charley if he knew whose child she really was. Her father had a deadly habit of turning on people as he had turned on her own mother who had run away. Marcus Sheffield was a very bad loser.

These were Suzannah's thoughts as she rode her beautiful mare, Gypsy, through the cool rustling woods by the river. She loved this horse so much it quietened her mind

just to be up on her back. Finally they were out from
under the trees and she huddled over Gypsy's neck and
let her do what she loved best. Gallop. The wind
streamed past them, fragrant, sun polished, offering little
resistance to horse and rider. Once a long, low branch
whipped Suzannah's back but nothing could detract from
the matchless pleasure of streaking across the gilded
grasslands. Gypsy's flying hooves kicked up tussocks
decorated with a crush of wild flowers. There was nothing the mare wouldn't do for her. Take fences with soaring leaps, obey her every command. Gypsy was a great
horse. There was no way she could sell her, though a few
people knowing their reduced circumstances had made
substantial offers. She would sell every piece of jewellery
she possessed before she would part with that mare. The
Schroeders, good people that they were, were keeping
Gypsy on their farm, putting her out to soft spring pas-
ture, refusing all payment.

"You looked out for us. Now it's our turn to look out
for you," Mrs Schroeder had told her quietly. Suzannah
truly didn't know what she had done, not realising the
warmth and friendliness of her manner all through the
years. The Easter and Christmas gifts she arranged com-
pensated for Marcus Sheffield's patronising attitude with
everyone in his employ. Many people in the town weren't
that unhappy when Marcus Sheffield "came a cropper".
He was too much the snob, too high-handed in his dealings. Suzannah was different. Brimming through with the
joy of life. *Until* her marriage when she seemed to quiet
down, the old vitality dimmed. It was pretty much evident to most people that her father had pushed her into
marriage with one of their own kind. A devil's bargain
when the young Nick Konrads had disappeared from the
town overnight. No one knew, as yet, he was the new

owner of Bellemont, but gossip fairly crackled since he had
been spotted at Martin White's funeral, then a short time
later talking to Suzannah and her little girl outside Charlotte's
school. Hans Schroeder, never slow-witted, had his own the-
ories, which he discussed with his wife. In his opinion Nick
Konrads, a clever young man Hans had admired openly,
treated so badly by Marcus Sheffield, had returned like an
avenging angel. It wasn't an extravagant fancy, either.

Adrienne wasted no time putting a private investigator to
work. It took two days for the investigator, a woman, to
come up with a great deal of information. All through
their high school days and later when they were at university, Suzannah Sheffield and Nick Konrads had been
inseparable. Suzannah and Nick was the way it went.
Most people doubted Suzannah's father was happy about
it, but the whole town felt marriage between the two of
them was inevitable at some stage. Everyone knew as
well that Martin White was in love with Suzannah.
Martin, too, was a part of her life, always running when-
ever she beckoned. They had grown even closer after
Suzannah had returned home leaving Nick Konrads still
studying in Sydney. Not that Suzannah had ever really
turned to Martin. It was simply that he and his sisters
were her close childhood friends. There was a strange
episode shortly after Nick Konrads returned to town after
gaining a brilliant degree. In his absence battle lines had
been drawn. Marcus Sheffield and his hand-picked pro-
spective son-in-law, Martin, on one side, the migrant boy
made good on the other. An old friend of Suzannah's
through high school told the investigator Suzannah was
often in tears about the complete alienation between her
father and Nick. She said once in a moment of despair

her father was "running her life". Very few people had been coerced to speak. The whole story came tumbling out as though people were anxious to get the story straight in their own minds. The town had never forgotten Nick Konrads's strange disappearance, then shortly afterwards Suzannah Sheffield's marriage to Martin White. That was the part that really mystified everyone. The whole town knew she had given her heart to Nick. He had never been an ordinary sort of boy or young man. No one was surprised when he became so marvellously successful in a highly competitive world. They were proud. The investigator found out a great deal without arousing too many suspicions. That came later. She heard about the enormous party Marcus Sheffield threw to celebrate the birth of his first grandchild, Charlotte Marie-Louise Sheffield-White. She heard about Martin White's tragic death. Adrienne pored over the dossier, absorbed in it totally. Afterwards it seemed to her the best person to act as catalyst would be the father. Marcus Sheffield had hated Nick once. God knows how he would react when he found out Nick Konrads and not Martin had fathered his grandchild. It meant nothing to Adrienne that Marcus Sheffield was ill. Her agenda was to create as much trouble as she could.

Less than a week later Marcus Sheffield walked down to the letter box to collect the morning's mail. Suzannah, who usually did it, had gone into town to do some shopping so he had the house to himself until around one, when Suzannah had promised to return to get his lunch. They'd had to let Dorothy, their long-time housekeeper at Bellemont, go. Suzannah did everything now but she appeared to be taking it easily in her stride. He didn't like all this talk about her going off to find a job. The Sheffield women had never worked except to chair committees in town. Besides he was afraid of what he might do if Suzannah weren't around. He was frustrated beyond belief with his reduced state.

He collected the mail, mostly for Suzannah. Sympathy cards were still coming in from all over. One letter for him. He waited until he was back on the porch to read it. The porch had slender white columns wreathed with jasmine. He wasn't quite sure he liked it. The scent in the bright sunshine was almost overpowering. Marcus Sheffield opened the letter tentatively, which was far from his way, but for some reason he sensed something dire in the contents.

It was short. Very short really. All set down in black and white. His perfect grandchild, the very image of her mother, was what he had always shrunk from. The skeleton in the closet. Charlotte was Nick Konrads's child. The writer, anonymous of course, gutless wonder, he felt sure he knew the gender, had seen proof positive. DNA testing. He, Marcus Sheffield, could delve into the rest.

He felt none of the red rage he once might have experienced. For the first time he began to feel horror at himself. Horror at what he had done. His beloved Suzannah had loved Konrads so much yet he had wrecked her chance of happiness by removing Konrads from her life. He could never begin to make it up to her. And Martin! Poor weak Martin who had allowed himself to be used so that at the end of the day he would win Suzannah for his own. Charley with her radiant presence and huge blue-green eyes. The truth be known he had always felt a little discomfited by those eyes. The one feature he couldn't readily identify in either family. Now he remembered the small, quiet woman who had been Nick Konrads's mother. For all Suzannah had been in and out of the Konrads' house as a child, he had usually sent someone to pick her up in the Rolls or on occasions gone himself giving Mrs Konrads on the verandah a casual wave. Now he remembered the light-filled eyes. Eyes one saw even from a distance.

He had tried to play God.

Marcus Sheffield felt a great rush of physical nausea. He stumbled back into the house, feeling a peculiar sensation start up in his head. A kind of terrible meltdown like his brain was turning to treacle. He really didn't know if he was going to see Suzannah and Charley again. He desperately needed to wash away his sins.

He broke the speed limit driving to Ashbury, taking the quiet country backroads, handling the big car with his usual skill even as he felt pierced through with remorse. Suzannah had rung him, hysterical as he had never heard her, accusing him of pure cruelty. Her father had suffered another stroke after reading his letter. While his heart lunged in perplexity and shock, thinking Marcus Sheffield dead, Suzannah told him in a broken-hearted voice he had been taken to hospital and was now in intensive care.

"How could you do it, Nick?" she cried. "Is your hate so implacable?"

It had been useless trying to deny all knowledge of what she was saying. He had sent no letter. That wasn't *his* way. But she was too far gone to hear. Instead he told her he was coming.

"There's nothing you can do. Nothing! You've done it all." She hung up on him.

This time, feeling queer and upset, he decided he wasn't going to take the blame. Someone was playing a dangerous game. Someone, it seemed, who knew all about the DNA report. Incredible to think it could be anyone on his staff, though all of them had access to his office. No one really knew anything about his background. He trusted Bebe with his life. As he worked his way through names he came to consider Adrienne. Adrienne drowning in jealousy, letting herself believe she was the classic scorned woman. It was a bit rich to think Adrienne could have done such a thing. And yet! He had seen an awful lot in his life. Furious emotions that changed people, forcing them into making terrible mistakes.

When he arrived at the cottage, just on dusk, a strange woman part-opened the door to him, a hesitant half smile on her motherly face.

"Yes?"

"I'd like to speak to Mrs White," he said pleasantly. "Is she at home?"

"I'm afraid she isn't." The woman broke off to look back over her shoulder as small footsteps clattered in the hallway. "It's all right, Charlotte, I'll attend to this, dear."

"But it's Mr Konrads," a child's voice piped. "Mummy would want him to come in. He's a good friend of ours."

"Really?" The woman, a relative newcomer to the town who lived only a few doors down, opened the door further so Charlotte could run to the strikingly handsome man standing on the porch. He looked enormously respectable, very tall as he stood framed in the doorway, the aura of money and power clinging to him.

"Charlotte, how are you?" Nick broke into a smile, the giant weight around his heart easing at the sight of his child.

"I'm all right but Mummy's terrible," Charley whispered confidentially, moving to take him sweetly by the hand. "Won't you come in and wait?"

"Yes, please do." Suzannah's neighbour murmured, feeling somewhat outmanoeuvred by the child. She moved away so their visitor and Charlotte could come through the doorway. "Mrs White should be on her way home from the hospital now," she told him. "Could I get you something?"

He looked at her gratefully. He hadn't eaten since breakfast. "Coffee would be nice. Black."

"I'll get it." She left them both sitting in the living room.

"Grandpa is sick again," Charley confided, moving closer. "They had to take him to hospital in an ambulance. I was at school."

"I'm sorry to hear that, Charlotte." He responded with tenderness, not wanting to stare at her, his heart lifting with pride. She spoke beautifully. She was clearly very intelligent.

"I get lots of little taunts at school," she said, distress in her voice.

He frowned. "What about?"

This time the distress was evident in her small heart-shaped face. "Did you hear we've lost all our money?"

He found himself taking her hand. "Money isn't everything in the world, Charlotte. It's what's in your mind and your heart that really counts. The nicest people, the ones I've liked most, haven't had a lot of money like your grandfather. But I know it makes you sad to be away from Bellemont."

She nodded, not pulling away but sitting comfortably hand in hand. "Mummy told me you own it now."

"And I promise you I'll look after it," he said gently.

"It would mean a lot to me, Charlotte, if you would come visit me. We could go riding, I know you own a pony."

"Lady." Charley's face was wreathed in smiles. "Do you know Mr Schroeder?"

"Yes, I do. I used to do lots of jobs for him."

"He's keeping Gypsy," Charley said. "That's Mummy's horse, and Lady on his farm. He's a very nice man and Mrs Schroeder is lovely. Are you going to live at Bellemont?" She looked at him with absolute pleasure in her eyes.

"I can't live there, Charlotte," he said. "I have a business in Sydney to run. It takes up most of my time. But I'm hoping to get away at weekends."

"I'm hoping you'll want to stay. Are you going to give Mr Schroeder his job back?"

"You think I should?" He sat on the sofa, just drinking her in.

"Oh, yes! Mr Schroeder knows all about growing grapes and making wine. Kurt, his son, has to work for the town council now when he should be making wine. That's what Mummy said. I know Mummy hated it when they lost their jobs at Bellemont."

"You leave it to me." Nick smiled into his daughter's eyes.

"I knew you'd help," Charley said earnestly.

Beverley, Charley's minder, returned with a tray, setting it down on the coffee table. The wonderful aroma of coffee, still in the plunger, pervaded the air; a cup and saucer, sugar in a silver bowl, a glass of chocolate milk for Charley, a selection of homemade biscuits. Beverley, a good cook, had made them for Suzannah.

"Gosh, this is like a party." Charley gave a little giggle. "Aren't you going to have anything, Beverley?"

"No, thank you, dear." Beverley smiled at the child,

showing her affection. "I'll wait until Mummy comes home, then I'll go."

Suzannah pulled into the driveway a short time later, the blood surging against her eardrums as she recognised Nick's car.

So he had come. Wasn't that Nick's way? When he said he was going to do something, he did it. Like making her and her father pay. Hurriedly she got out of the car, slamming the door shut. It was obvious he was making himself comfortable inside. Such was his incredible power he had won over his daughter at first sight. The tender-hearted Beverley wouldn't have stood a chance. She'd have let him in. Keeping herself together was critical. She couldn't upset Charley, or let her nice neighbour become aware of her seething emotions. Nick had handed down his vengeance in full measure. Her father was in a coma in intensive care. The shocking letter Nick had sent him was crushed up in her handbag.

Wildness ran in her veins. Wildness and frustration. By the time she reached the front door Charley was there, Beverley hovering behind her. Charley was incandescent with pleasure, her small face animated by the need to give her mother the good news.

"Mummy, Mr Konrads is here," she announced, sounding thrilled. "He's come to see how Grandpa is. Is Grandad a lot better?"

How could she frighten her? Charley had had enough frights in her short life. "Grandpa is in intensive care, darling," she said gently. "He's being well looked after but there has been no change."

Though Suzannah was striving for composure, Beverley, too recently a widow, saw through to the underlying anxiety. "Is there anything more I can do for you, Suzannah?'' she said. ''I'm quite happy to take Charley down to my place while you have a talk to your friend.'' There could be serious things that had to be said without upsetting the child, Beverley reasoned. Mr Sheffield could well die. Like her Neville.

It was a way out. Suzannah whirled about as Nick walked into the hallway, the overhead light shimmering over his black hair and his strong bone structure. His eyes seemed to blaze with high emotion and danger.

''Suzannah,'' he said in a grave voice, ''I had to come.''

Charley hugged her mother's hips tightly. ''Grandpa *is* all right, isn't he?''

What could she say. Grandad didn't have a chance? ''We must say our prayers,'' she answered, her face softening as she looked down at her child. ''Would you mind going with Beverley for ten minutes, darling, while I speak to Mr Konrads?'' She kept her voice calm while inside she was shivering with nerves.

''Can't I stay?'' Charley started to look worried.

''I'll come down and fetch you,'' Nick promised, moving closer. ''Your mother and I have grown-up things to discuss, Charlotte. Nothing at all for you to worry about.''

He flashed her his quite wonderful smile so Beverley wasn't surprised when the little girl caught her hand. ''You can tell me all about the stars,'' Charley suggested. ''I love to look up at them twinkling in the sky.''

''They've been twinkling for many billions of years,'' he told her lightly. ''The same stars we look at tonight shone down on Cleopatra, Alexander the Great, Darius of Persia, the infant Jesus at Bethlehem. I'll point out the constellation Orion, the mighty hunter, where new stars have come to life in the last fifty years. I'll explain to you how a star takes shape, if you like.''

''That will be wonderful!'' Charley breathed, her cheeks flaming with rose colour.

Suzannah stood very quietly until the footsteps had died away, then she burst into desperate speech. ''What are you trying to do, Nick? Take my daughter from me? I know all about your charm.''

''Make that *our* daughter,'' he said, catching hold of her by the arm as she tried to whirl past him. ''I didn't send any letter to your father, Suzannah. I won't say that one more time. But I know exactly what was in it. You can't get away with any more lies.'' He ignored her moan. ''I have irrefutable proof Charlotte is my child. You know it. I know it. Now your father knows it. Plus the person who devoted their time to exposing the truth for their own ends.''

''I'm supposed to believe that?'' The breath shook in Suzannah's throat. She jerked her arm away and moved into the living room, turning to confront him.

''Above all you believe what you *want* to believe,'' he said harshly. ''It's a handy trick hiding from the truth. Keeping quiet. Saying nothing. Ultimately, however, the truth will out. Charlotte is my child and I'm here to claim her.''

She was certain of it. ''And what about *me?*''

''You're not denying it then?'' His black gaze whipped over her.

''How could I in the face of your evidence. It broke my father. *He* couldn't face it. I came home to find him unconscious on the floor.'' Her willowy body was bowed by pain.

The sight shafted him. ''I'm sorry, Suzannah. I'm sorry that had to happen but it was none of my doing. Your father can't really love Charlotte if he can reject her because she's my child. Charlotte is a little person in her own right. She has her own personality and character.''

Suzannah moved blindly into an armchair. ''He probably won't want to see he again. That's if he survives.''

Nick took a moment to get his own feelings under control. ''You're only surmising that. I well remember how he adored you. That feeling would have extended to your child.''

''So why did he have another stroke?'' she asked urgently, raising her violet eyes to him.

He moved to sit near her, wrapped around by her scent and her presence. ''Suzannah, you must know follow-up strokes are common. I'm not saying the news wouldn't have been a *shock*.''

''So where did the informant get this information from?'' she asked in bitter challenge. ''Surely it's highly confidential?''

''It is.'' He fisted his hand so he wouldn't touch her. ''I received confirmation at my office. I thought it was safe.''

''Are you trying to tell me it was someone in your office?'' she asked with barely suppressed fury.

He shook his head. ''None of them is capable of such treachery.''

''So *who?*'' she demanded. The pain would never be wiped away.

''I have my suspicions, Suzannah.'' His voice was taut. ''I'll take care of it.''

She gave a scathing laugh for reply. ''Do you think that gives me any feeling of security, of privacy? You didn't take care of it last time. Someone read your confidential correspondence, Nick. Someone had the cruelty to pass on the news. Rattle the cage as it were. Someone who didn't care about the consequences."

"I regret it profoundly," he said, fighting the compulsion to go to her and pull her into his arms. Whether he wanted it or not his need for her was endless.

"My father might die." Tears welled like jewels in her eyes.

"I don't think he would care to live in a badly diminished state," he offered quietly, grieved by everything that had happened.

She stood up and took tempestuous steps away from him, her breasts moving in agitation against the thin dark blue silk of her blouse. "I wish we'd never met," she said fiercely, all her senses soaring out of control. "I wish we'd never grown up together. I wish I'd never loved you."

He stood up, went to her, then pulled her body back against him, the cloud of her hair tickling his chin. "Everyone I know of has regrets, Suzannah. You're not alone. There was no good reason my mother should have died in her mid-fifties. Does one die of a broken heart? Don't look at it from your own point of view. Your father engineered his own ruin. Maybe Martin's, too. You said yourself Martin had to confess to what he'd done to me. I might never have known Charlotte is my daughter had not Martin been killed. Things might have been very different if *you'd* shown a little guts."

She spun in his arms so alight with anger her eyes sparkled like sapphires. "I think you'd better check that out. Like you've checked out everything else. I've had plenty of guts. What do you think it's been like for me these past years?"

He stared down into her lovely overwrought face.

"You married Martin," he said grimly. "You made no attempt to get away."

"I was pregnant with your child, damn you." A passionate fury ran through her.

"You couldn't *tell* me?" he demanded. "You couldn't face me? God Almighty, Suzannah, I loved you with all my heart. I would never had abandoned you. I would have adored it to know you were with child. Do you understand?" He took her delicate shoulders beneath his strong hands and shook her.

"And what would we have done for money? How would we have lived? You were only just out of university, remember?" She realised she feared him every bit as much as she loved him. Nick was quite capable of instigating a custody battle.

"I've always known how to earn money," he answered with contempt. "We could have gone to my mother for support. She would never have refused whatever help she could give us. Can't you fathom what a crime it was to deprive her of her grandchild? A child, moreover, with her own eyes. And there's something about Charley's laugh, the way she spreads her fingers over yours."

She tried to ease back, straining the curve of her neck but he held her fast. "All right, I was a coward," she flared. "I should have told your mother I was pregnant but I was crazy with worry. My father would have been shocked out of his mind. He was always so proud of me he could have shown me the door. Your mother didn't really want to see me again. She made it plain. It was my fault you were banished from the town."

"What was she supposed to do?" He gripped her more tightly, listening to her ragged little breaths. "You abused her trust. What your father and Martin did was vile."

"But you got to have your revenge." Her voice was so brittle she didn't recognise it as her own.

"And the revenge isn't done." His eyes narrowed. "I may not be able to take Charlotte from you. I care too much about her, but you're not going to be able to take her from me, either."

"So what are you going to do?" She stared up into his eyes. "Ruin my reputation in this town? Take it out on Charley? Already some of the children make little taunts."

"I think you *know* the answer," he said.

"No, *tell* me." She threw up her gleaming head.

"In another six or seven months—I'm not prepared to wait any longer—you're going to marry me, Suzannah," he said, with a fierce desire that had nothing to do with love.

"Oh, please, and bring more unhappiness into my life?" she jeered, desperately wishing things were different.

"Charlotte is mine and so are you." His dominant dark face was set. "Your protestations make no difference. I want you both."

Along with the implacability ran a deep sensuality. "Is this what you call hammering out a deal?" she gasped.

"It's as much for Charlotte as anyone else. She barely knows me but already I'm important to her. I love her pure and simple and I want to protect and enfold her. I want to give her all the good things in life. I want to give her back Bellemont. For herself and her heirs. I want her to make her home with *both* her parents. I won't stand by and allow you to remarry some time in the future. A woman as young and beautiful as you would surely do that."

"You can't force me into any of this," Suzannah said, her seeming anger offset by longings. "You may be able to prove you're Charlotte's father but there's no court in the world that would say I have to marry you to keep her.''

"Suzannah, I'm not a man to be trifled with. You *know* what you must do. If poor Martin had serious feelings of guilt, so must you. You surely don't want me to tell Charlotte she's my daughter?''

She could feel the heat rise under her skin. "There's no way she would understand. She's only a baby.''

"She'd understand all right,'' he rasped, "but I would never tell her until the time is right. Think carefully before you answer. You *will* marry me.''

"I don't see that as a question.'' Her voice almost broke.

"It isn't, but I'd be obliged if you'd answer.''

"When you're going to punish me for the rest of my life?''

"On the contrary. I intend to take good care of you and of course my daughter. Your father, too, if he survives.''

This was all her own fault. Retribution. "Damn you, Nick,'' she muttered, her throat working. "Damn you for going off and leaving me.''

"And damn you for lying to me,'' he replied. "Curses aren't terribly comfortable, are they? Shall we seal our agreement with a kiss?''

The hard mockery of his tone further infuriated her. "Why would you want a woman who no longer loves you?'' she said bleakly, hoping no part of her heart showed in her eyes.

"I think I can handle it.'' His voice was suave. "I know there's a difference between love and *sex* but there's still plenty of *that* on both sides. Maybe I should prove it.''

She thought she would have broken away, only his arms held her so tightly. She felt terribly vulnerable, defenceless against his male strength and strong will. Worse, she wouldn't have him know how much she wanted him, how life without him had been wasted.

He parted her lovely full mouth easily with his, his own fevered with a powerful desire he didn't bother to hide. He wanted her to understand once and for all she was *his*. His hands slid deeply, rhymically, possessively, over her back, arching her to him. How many times had he dreamed of this? How many times had he tossed and turned in his dream-clogged sleep longing for one traitorous woman who invaded his mind? A woman Martin White had tricked into his bed. How had he let that happen? Anger and frustration increased his desire, heating his blood. He wanted to swoop her up, tumble her into his car, drive madly through the night overtaking all others until he was home again in his own apartment doing all the things to her he had done in his sleeping fantasies.

Her breasts swelled beneath his questing hand, even the silk seemed electrified by his touch. He could feel the shivery ripples run through her body, reinforcing his own enormous desire. In a moment, he felt he would reach a point too close to the edge.

Lifting his mouth from hers was a strangely ravishing agony. "Convinced?" His voice mocked when he knew a painful yearning for all he had lost.

"So? You always had the capacity to drive me off the deep end." She shook her head sadly.

"Isn't it odd then that I didn't take it? I could have had you from the day you turned thirteen and gave off femininity like some wonderful erotic scent. I didn't touch you. I couldn't. Not for all the temptation, because I would have despised myself. I cared about you too much. I wanted to marry you. There was never anyone else.''

Her heart broke over. ''And you made me pregnant that one time when we were alone in the house. It doesn't seem possible. I took no steps to prevent it but I could never conceive with Martin.''

A terrible jealousy caught him exposed. ''I don't want to talk about Martin and your marriage. That's the *past*. Lock it away like you locked me out of your heart.'' He drew away from her abruptly and turned to the door. ''I'd better go collect Charlotte, then I'll drive out to Bellemont. Ring me if you hear from the hospital overnight. I don't care what time it is. If he gets through the night I'll call in tomorrow. I've got to go back. I'm finishing off a very important program. When that's accomplished we have to talk further. I don't want you and Charlotte here when Bellemont is standing empty.''

She fixed her lustrous stare on him. ''Wouldn't that ensure a lot of talk? Charley and I would have to confront it.''

''You can dream up the right response,'' he countered. ''There are very many things you can do for me, Suzannah. You said you needed a job. You're the ideal person to run Bellemont in my absence. I'm reopening the vineyard, modernising the winery, extending the planting. Maybe Chardonnay, Semillon, we can discuss that. The Schroeders will come back. We'll need staff. For the house, the vineyard, the winery, the gardens. You can attend to all that. I have plans for the stables, too. I want the ordinary kids of this district, not just the rich kids, to be taught how to ride properly. We can run a school. I know you'd like to get started on that. Hire the right people. We can provide quality horses for accomplished riders, get Gypsy and Lady back from Hans. Bellemont will return to being a working farm.''

''And you'd put all this in my hands?'' She tried to keep the incredulous note out of her voice.

''Why not?'' he said tersely. ''You've had plenty of training. Life with me won't be so bad, Suzannah. That's if you don't mess it up.''

# CHAPTER SIX

ADRIENNE had little scientific knowledge. She did not fully understand that fingerprints could be matched up nor did she take into account the important connections he had made through his work. As with the DNA it was a simple matter to have his suspicions confirmed. Adrienne had indeed sent the letter to Marcus Sheffield. He confronted her with it in her office, watching her cheeks splotch with red.

"Didn't you think for one moment the shock might have killed him?" he asked.

Adrienne attempted a laugh. "I heard he was a tough old bird. I would have thought you'd be only too pleased to see him get his comeuppance, Nick, considering what he did to you."

Had she checked on him? Did it matter? "Well then, you'd better tell me. What exactly did he do?"

"Come off it, Nick," she jeered. "You check up on me. I check up on you. You have to grow a thick skin in this world."

"You mean you set some investigator to work?"

"Well I couldn't go down there myself," she retorted, sitting back in her chair. "Like you, I have to run a business."

"But what was the point of it all?" he asked, standing, staring down at her.

"You don't think I was going to allow you to disappear from my life?" she said in an incredulous tone.

*"Allow?"* He honed in on that. "That's an odd word. You have no control over *me*."

She literally wrung her hands. "You mustn't go back to that woman, Nick. As far as I can make out she's been responsible for most of the unhappiness in your life."

He controlled his anger, told himself to sit down. "So you thought if you wrote to her father her father could sway her again?"

"Why not?" she retorted, still with hope in her voice. "These old families loathe scandal. What about the grandparents on the other side, Nick? Have you thought of them? The people who think your child is part of *their* family. All they have left of their son. Isn't that the way it goes?"

He stared at her in total silence, then with a horrendous understanding. "I had no idea you'd become so obsessive."

"Why would you?" she countered bitterly. "I did my best to keep it hidden. Anyway, don't talk to me about *obsession*, Nick. It's got its great claws into you."

"So you mustn't try to rescue me, Adrienne," he warned. "It was a cruel thing you did sending that letter to Marcus Sheffield. He may not die but he'll be confined to a wheelchair, paralysed down the left side of his body. He hasn't regained his speech. He may never. Doesn't that fill you with deep regret?"

She blushed deeply again. "Don't be ridiculous, Nick. I don't know the man."

"And to think I thought you had some capacity for heart."

She sat bolt upright, fixing her amber eyes on his. "The only one I care about is *you*. Even my mother used to say I'm as tough as an old boot. Listen, darling, you have to stop feeling sorry for these people. Concentrate

on the wrong they did you. I understand totally and con-
done your ambition to get square. You've done it now.
You've gone to some pains to acquire their old ancestral
home. Bravo! It must have come as a tremendous bomb-
shell when they found out.''

"I suppose it did.'' No way he could deny it. "But I
would never have sent Marcus Sheffield your anonymous
letter. Not when his health was already broken. You've
destroyed our friendship, Adrienne, as surely as if you'd
hacked it to pieces with a knife. I won't be seeing you
again.'' He stood up, full of a sad disgust, watching
Adrienne come feverishly around her desk, her eyes very
bright.

"Have you the smallest inkling how much I love
you?'' she asked, clutching at the lapels of his suit jacket.

"If I lost my company, Adrienne, you wouldn't love
me at all.'' He spoke dryly.

"But you're not going to do that. You're way too
clever. No, Nick, you're on a flight to the stars. That's if
you don't destroy yourself going back to this woman.
God knows she made her husband unhappy enough.''

It was startling how much she had learned. "It's easy
enough to become unhappy when one loses all self-
esteem,'' he said sombrely. "I'm sorry if you've been
hurt, Adrienne, but I have to tell you I'm appalled by
your behaviour. You'd be wise not to interfere in my life
again.''

As formidable as he looked, Adrienne didn't shrink.
"You'll come back to me,'' she insisted on a mournful
note. "It's her *home,* after all, your Suzannah cares about.
Bellemont. Her home and her haven. I'd love it, too, if
I'd been born in such a place. But no such luck. I've had
to work damned hard for what I've got in this world.
Your Suzannah married a man she didn't love so she

wouldn't have to leave the family mansion. She rejected you because her father probably threatened to disinherit her. Now you're rich enough to give her back what she wants. But just remember, Nick, Bellemont comes first.''

There was an element of truth in it, he thought. Love of Bellemont ran generations deep. His own little daughter knew her roots. From that moment on the thought was always with him.

Such was the irony of life it was Nick's money that paid for her father's care. Marcus Sheffield was shifted from hospital into an exclusive nursing home on the outskirts of town where he had around-the-clock attention. Physiotherapists worked on him in intensive sessions to the extent he regained most of the mobility in his limbs but his speech remained badly impaired. Nevertheless he was mentally alert and had no difficulty recognising Suzannah and Charlotte. Suzannah called in on her father each day, sitting quietly with him, whether he was asleep or awake, holding his hand.

"You're so good to him, dear," Carol Williams, his private nurse, told her approvingly. "Such a comfort. It's easy to see how much he loves you."

She took Charlotte frequently, mostly for a short time after school. Marcus Sheffield's faded eyes followed the child as she moved quietly around the room, arranging things to please him. The lovely flowers Mummy always brought, little personal things from home, his silver-backed brushes, family photos in silver frames, a painting on the wall, lovely silk rugs to make Grandpa feel more at home. Often she spent her time sitting at her grandfather's feet as he sat in his wheelchair, one of his trembling hands resting lightly on her shoulder. She never complained, never tried to move away. Grandpa had written on his pad, the one he used to tell people what he meant, he "adored her". She was his favourite little girl in all the world. It made Charlotte feel happy even when she felt bad. It was so sad to see Grandpa so thin and old. So sad not to hear his big deep voice even though it used to boom at her.

Strangely it was a time of peace and reconciliation, these hours when all three of them sat quietly having conversations in their minds. If Suzannah had ever feared her father would turn on Charley now that he knew Nick was her father, the very opposite had happened. They had never seemed closer. The little girl all loving attentiveness, her grandfather holding back tears when she was leaving.

When Nick came down one weekend, Suzannah mentioned it to him.

"Speak to his doctors, see what they think. If they believe good quality home care can be managed, I don't see why he can't move back into Bellemont. He would need his private nurse on a full-time basis. It would establish a good reason for you and Charlotte to live there." This was said very dryly as Suzannah, a little frightened of what it might entail, had stayed on in the cottage.

Suzannah wondered what her father would make of Nick's amazingly generous offer. Reject it? But he did not. More than anything he wanted to see Bellemont once again.

It was not to happen. As preparations were underway, essential changes made at the house, Marcus Sheffield passed away in his sleep. On his bedside table lay his communicating pad and pen.

The last message read: Forgive me I was wrong.

It was the beginning of December now, a few more

weeks to Christmas, the festive season, the time to be at peace with the world. Yet Suzannah could not pull herself out of her depression. She tried very hard to be cheerful in front of Charley, who was home on the summer vacation, but Charley was very sensitive to her mother's pain.

When Suzannah saw her little daughter hiding away in the garden, quietly wiping her wet face on her sleeve, she felt a great wave of protective love. Charley, too, had been deprived of her loved ones, her grandfather and the man she had been reared to believe was her father. She would have to shake herself out of her own terrible lethargy and take control. Both of them were feeling Nick's continuing absence. He had flown to California on business. Almost two weeks had passed since he had come down to Bellemont, though they still lived in the cottage where Suzannah felt her father's lingering presence. A breathing space, she reasoned, before the return to her beloved Bellemont.

She began the task of recruiting and in many cases re-recruiting staff. Finally the very nature of the task convinced her the best place to operate from was Bellemont itself. Nick, on his return, rang her frequently but to all intents and purposes theirs might have been a business arrangement, never a partnership, let alone a relationship between two people who intended to marry primarily, it seemed, for the sake of their child. Nick was the boss. She was the valued employee and she had to admit he made her feel valued. It wasn't simply that he had wonderful skills when it came to handling people. He expected a great deal, challenging one's own ability to get on with the job. But he was unstinting in his praise when she moved all the right people into position. Of recent times he had come to asking for Charley to be put on the phone as well, amusing her with his conversation so that Charley always got off the phone laughing.

"I love Nick so much," she told her mother, rolling her eyes in a child's delight. "He makes me feel so happy!"

"Yes, Nick's good at doing that." Suzannah always turned away before Charley saw her sad expression. The future was looking rosy but she knew full well she would have to atone for the past.

Nick rang fairly late one evening, causing Suzannah to awake in panic, her breath shaking in her chest. She had retired earlier than usual after a long, busy day walking the vineyards with Hans and Kurt discussing their combined plans. Nick wanted more acres planted with vines, some four thousand semillon, the major white table wine variety of Australia and later, as an experiment, some three thousand vines of Sauvignon Blanc. Hans and Kurt had found Nick's plans inspirational, raising not a murmur against Nick's decision to bring in a brilliant young oenology graduate and grandson of a family with extensive viticultural experience. As well, in the afternoon she had to interview several applicants to take over the running of the riding school. Two men, four women, all with the right background and skills and so enthusiastic to get started she scarcely knew whom to pick. She had fallen asleep instantly, too tired out to be haunted by dreams, but the strident sound of the phone cutting into the night brought back stark memories. She was perpetually in anguish about Martin. Even though he and her father had virtually coerced her into marriage she was sick with combined regrets.

Consequently her voice was low and husky, carrying emotional fright. "Bellemont Farm. May I help you?"

"Did I wake you?" Nick asked.

"Yes." She sat up, leaning over to switch on the bedside lamp, a bronze figure of a beautiful winged nymph holding up a Nile-green fringed shade. Nick had found it in an out-of-the-way antique shop, repaired its broken wing beautifully and given it to her for her sixteenth birthday. In a houseful of superb antiques she treasured it.

"You sound like you're in pain or frightened?" His vibrant voice came across the wires with such immediacy he might have been with her in the room.

How well he knew her! "No, just an early night," she said evasively. "I'll go back to sleep after my report to you. The paddocks are ploughed. The posts, wire and irrigation lines in place. All we need now are workers to do the actual planting and fit up the vine guards."

"Fine." He brushed that aside. "But let's get back to you. You sound far from happy."

"On the basis of a few spoken words, Nick?"

"You forget I know you too well. Every nuance in your voice."

It was an odd time for her to long for him, for the power of his flesh.

"I'm still in mourning, Nick," she pointed out.

"Of course. We must have time for our grief," he answered. "But you shouldn't be alone. I'm coming as soon as I can. In fact, I've put together a team to join the locals in the planting. My own people from the company. Friends. A weekend affair. How do you feel about organising it?"

She had learned early how to play hostess. "When are

we talking about, Nick?'' she asked, sitting straighter in the bed, her mind already working on the idea.

''I thought Hans wanted to start the planting as soon as possible?''

''The preparation is complete. Richer soils are on the top of the ridges, deep sandy loams in the valley. No problem. The planting pattern has been decided on, uniform vine spacing, long straight rows. A good turning space at the end. We've taken everything into consideration.

''So what about this weeekend?'' he asked. ''It's Tuesday tomorrow. Enough time? I want you to take charge of everything. Organisation side of it, of course. I expect you to hire people to help out. Caterers, etc. I know you won't want me to make it *obvious* you're my hostess, neither do I want you to play down your place in the scheme of things. I want Charlotte to enjoy herself as well. Perhaps she could ask along some of her little friends. Make it a community affair. Let the people of the district join in.''

Pleasure leapt into her troubled mind, so she tumbled back against the pillows. ''I'm sure I can pull it all together.''

''I know you can,'' he said in a soft, smooth voice. ''You scared the daylights out of me when you were eight years old. Poised enough, imperious enough to be a little princess. I don't think I've ever been so much in awe of anyone in my life.''

Like a miracle the years fell away. ''Didn't I ever tell you I was scared of you, too?'' she retorted, unaware her own voice had turned to honey. ''The way you stood, the way you moved, the way you spoke with this foreign accent. How wonderfully handsome you were, like a god from another planet. You weren't like any other child I ever knew. To this day I don't know anyone like you. Even as a boy you had enough in you to put my father on guard.''

"It took years for him to forbid you to see me," he said.

"He asked your forgiveness in the end, Nick," she told him gently.

"Maybe he was scared of what lay ahead?"

"Repentance doesn't catch up with all of us," she pointed out.

"I'll have to sleep on that."

It seemed wise to change the subject. "You'll have to let me know the numbers, male and female guests," she said, suddenly businesslike. "The women you've thrown over. I hope none of them is coming?" She had a sudden picture of the woman called Adrienne's staring, unblinking gaze. Nick had never told her who had sent the letter to her father but she felt she *knew*.

"The only one who has ever made the blood roar through my veins is you, Suzannah," he reminded her, holding her enthralled. "What are you wearing right now? Tell me."

Seduction over the phone. She glanced down at her pale yellow nightdress, a deep convulsive shiver running the length of her body. "Cotton pyjamas," she said perversely.

He laughed, such a terribly attractive sound. "You didn't even favour them when you were a child. No, Suzannah, I see you in a sheath of silk. The colour is soft and luminous. Maybe pink, maybe peach. It has thin little straps over the shoulders and the neckline dips low into your beautiful breasts. You wear nothing beneath it. If you stood up I could see right through it. I can see it lying in a soft pool at your feet. I can see myself worshipping your body, my little sacrificial lamb," he added with the familiar edge of mockery.

"Do you think we will ever love each other again the way we used to?" she asked, touched by fear.

There was a long silence, thick with images. "The last thing I want to do is hurt your feelings," he said.

"For God's sake!" She recovered in an instant. "I wouldn't want you to, Nick."

This time his low laugh was somewhat discordant. "Hating, loving, what's the difference," he said. "You claimed my soul a long time ago."

Charley was absolutely thrilled when she heard about what was planned.

"You mean I can ask Lucy and Amanda?" She clasped her arms around her mother's neck, naming her White "cousins".

"Certainly, darling, if they would like to come." Suzannah had spoken many times to her White in-laws, all of them had been close up until Martin's death, but she couldn't shake off the feeling they blamed her in some way for Martin's final disintegration, if not for the actual accident. It was only natural, she supposed. God knows what they would think when they learned, as they inevitably would, she had, for the best of reasons, pulled the wool over their eyes.

Charley was Nick's child. The older she got the more it began to show. She was so highly intelligent she stood out from the rest of the children. As well as being academic, she had artistic skills. She could draw, not as children usually did with bright crayons and stick people. She had a definite gift. Her piano teacher at school went around calling Charley her "little wunderkind". She could swim. She could ride. She could hold her own in conversations with adults. She had a way of turning her head, directing a questioning eyebrow. The baby rosebud mouth was taking on a new shape, with definite upraised edges. The sable dark hair out of its plaits was developing a deep wave. Suzannah's own hair, though thick with lots of bounce, was perfectly straight. Charley didn't have her hairline, either. Charley was developing Nick's pronounced widow's peak.

"Please God, *help me*." Suzannah, locked into a dilemma often prayed. "Forgive me for being such a failure." Failure was a word no one else had ever applied to Suzannah. She had been her father's hostess from an early age. She knew all about running things. Orchestrating functions at short notice, highly successful luncheons, dinner parties, gala evenings, balls, the humbler community get-together. Best of all she knew how to make people feel wonderfully comfortable. It was a role that suited her right down to the ground, a combination of natural friendliness and charm and years of making herself indispensable to a father who had to entertain a good deal.

Nick eventually rang back with his numbers. He'd invited ten people in all, equally divided between male and female guests. The unattached males would be happy to bunk in the staff quarters, which included the cottage attached to the stables. The rest could share the guest bedrooms if she could take in Charley for the night.

The sound of his voice embraced her, warming the frozen reaches of her heart. What was it about Nick that had always enveloped and welcomed her? She had felt his presence around her all these past years. Riding through the eucalypt-scented woods, down by the river, their special pool, looking up at the blazing stars. She had lost her heart to him in childhood. Given it into his hands using a child's instincts. She knew now a child's instincts were true. Charley had turned into Nick's arms as though she had known and loved him all her life. Like mother. Like daughter.

Organising every aspect of the weekend kept her so busy she had little time to dwell on the sad changes in her life. The townspeople were wonderfully enthusiastic, welcoming the prospect of doing the planting with the promise of an alfresco barbecue, which Suzannah intended to set up near the rose gardens. Historically Bellemont's beautiful rose gardens had always been a feature of the farm. The hundreds of bushes had been planted not only for their near year-long glory and wonderful perfume, but as an early warning system for the precious vines. The same diseases that attacked the vines showed up first in the rosebushes. Suzannah had thought as a child the roses were eternally looking after the grapes.

The busy period was good for Charley, too. Her normally high spirits bounced back as she rushed to and fro taking messages, trying to help her mother with numerous little jobs, watching enthralled as the big marquee was set up on the lawn, chatting on the phone to her "cousins" who were as excited about being a part of it all as Charley. In a sense she was running wild, free of the restraints her grandfather's illness and subsequent uncertain temper had imposed upon her. Suzannah saw no harm in it, rather it was a therapy as Charley returned to normal behaviour.

There was no need to call in professional caterers, either. Suzannah organised all the food and drink, calling on the excellent local produce as she had done so many times in the past. The women of the town would be on hand to help her. Every last one had offered their services including Martin's two sisters, who with their husbands would be helping to plant the new semillon vines.

It was almost like the old days, Suzannah thought. If only she could move her mind to another place. It seemed to be her lot to carry her burden of grief wherever she went, but she couldn't bear to inflict it on Charley.

Never had she wanted Nick more.

He and his friends swooped on her towards dusk Friday evening. Nick in his Jaguar with a woman passenger, a short plumpish very pleasant-looking person who had to be his devoted Bebe. The others whooping like contestants in a car rally leaping from Land Cruisers, all dressed alike in casual shirts and jeans. The evening sky was an intoxicating gauzy mauve but soon darkness would fall as theatrically as a theatre curtain.

While Charley ran on ahead, streaking like an arrow to Nick, who whirled her off the ground, Suzannah took a little time walking from the porch, down the short flight of stone stairs and out onto the driveway. Thank God the woman Adrienne wasn't there. Adrienne, she felt, was a woman who could hurt her. All the others were smiling happily, dispelling any feeling of awkwardness as though the exact reason for her presence was the last thing on their minds.

Nick reached her first, took her hand, then bent to kiss her cheek. "Come and say hello. Everyone's dying to meet you." He felt the slight tremble in her hand and tightened his grasp. She was wearing a flower embroidered summery dress in a shade of turquoise that turned her eyes into glittering jewels. She was so beautiful, so damned aristocratic, the blood swirled around through his veins so it became an actual ache. This woman who had such a profound capacity to hurt him.

Bebe, looking around her with some awe, the magnificent homestead, the gardens, the rolling hills and the green and gold vineyards, thought the young woman walking towards her, holding on to Nick's hand, was the answer to any man's prayers. She didn't need any confidence from Nick, either, to tell this was definitely the woman in his life. But there were many mysteries to ponder. For instance, why would a little girl who looked almost exactly like her mother remind Bebe of Nick? My goodness, there was a story there, Bebe thought.

The friendliness, the contagious enthusiasm made Suzannah expand with joy. Almost exclusively, with the exception of Bebe and a distinguished-looking older man, a professor, these were young people around her own age and she found their company fresh and uplifting. She'd had no time to recover from her family tragedies, both events had left permanent scars, but it was wonderful to look into so many smiling faces and see their instant approval and liking.

"You're a great hit!" Nick murmured, his arm around her shoulder as they all went into the house. "I knew you would be."

It took no time at all to fix everyone up happily with accommodation within the homestead itself. The young married couples together, single males, single females sharing. Bebe with a charming room overlooking the rose gardens to herself, Noel Geddes, a widower in his mid-fifties and one of Nick's early mentors next door. Suzannah had gained the impression Nick was promoting a romance between Bebe and Noel. She had noticed herself how the light came into Bebe's face every time Noel turned to speak to her. She wished them luck. Life was nothing without love.

"Isn't it wonderful!" Charley kept saying, dashing excitedly in and out of each room. "I love having visitors."

"That's a lovely little girl you've got there!" Bebe turned away from her rapt admiration of the rose gardens to smile at Suzannah. "So much like you and as bright as a button. She tells me she's going to play the piano for me before dinner."

"She's very capable, too." Suzannah smiled back, her eyes proclaiming the depth of her love. "But I'm not going to let her monopolise you, Bebe. So don't worry."

"As if she would. I love children," Bebe said. "Never married of course. I had a few offers but—"

"Nick did mention you have an invalid mother," Suzannah said sympathetically.

Bebe looked down at her ringless hands. "And I love her dearly. It's Nick who's made our lives incomparably easier. It was a great day I decided to cut loose from a go-nowhere safe job and follow Nick. He's a genius. Even better, he has the kindest heart imaginable."

Such a smile of sorrowing joy touched Suzannah's mouth, Bebe was both fascinated and perplexed. She knew the moment she saw Nick and Suzannah together they were hopelessly entwined. Yet how could this beautiful young creature with her heart-breaking smile, so obviously deeply affected by Nick, have married someone else?

Suzannah had arranged dinner as a buffet with the guests at ease wandering around the broad covered terrace with its overview of the floodlit swimming pool and on the far side of the meandering creek. They piled their plates high with delicious food, taking up positions on the circular tables that had been set up on the terrace or the inbuilt cushioned banquettes that surrounded the swimming pool on the lower level. The emphasis was on informality and soon the country landscape was echoing with laughter and the soothing music that filtered from the house.

Charley was ecstatic about being allowed up but by eight o'clock Suzannah grasped her by the hand and led her away to choruses of, "Night, night, Charley, sleep tight!"

"You'll come up, too, won't you?" Charley begged Nick as they encountered him in the hallway, her small face beseeching.

"Show the way!" He swept out a gallant hand, which further tickled Charley's sense of humour.

"Don't get her too excited, Nick," Suzannah murmured, as Nick folded the child into his arms.

"I want you to stay here forever, Nick," Charley said. "You're the very first person to carry me to my room except Mummy when I was little."

"Okay, but you're feeling a bit heavy." He pretended to stagger.

"Daddy never did," Charley said, giggling at Nick's antics. "A lot of time he used to forget about me."

At that, Nick's gaze fixed itself on Suzannah's dismayed face but he didn't say anything until Charley was safely tucked into bed, her eyes already closing.

Outside in the quiet corridor he took Suzannah's arm, spinning her to face him. "So Martin knew?"

She tried to step back but he manoeuvred her against the wall, the sconce above her throwing a light like golden sunshine all over her face. "He didn't. He just wasn't much good at demonstrating his affection."

"When he was literally crazy about you." He shook his head, disgusted. "When he wanted to crush me into the ground. Are you such a coward you can't tell me the truth?"

She looked up at his smouldering face, the contempt in it an unending heartache. "Don't tell me you intend to start an argument with your friends in the house?"

"Curiously, right at this moment, I don't care. Charlotte must have had a miserable time of it?"

Tell the truth when she felt so much guilt. "That's not right. My father doted on her. He doted on her right up until the end. Even when he knew Charley was your daughter."

"So much the better for him if he had to face his Maker," he rasped. "I'm talking about Martin. Did he love you and shut my daughter out?" Anger was so deep it refused to budge.

"I won't talk about this now, Nick," she protested, a pulse beating nervously in her throat. Why did anger provoke an erotic abyss? Underneath everything was her sexual longing for him.

"Because you don't dare?" he challenged her.

"Not when you're holding a pistol at my head."

He laughed; his beautiful mouth twisted. "If anyone was cruel it was you, Suzannah."

She could see the signs of his own fermenting desire. "You've got to stop this, Nick," she warned.

"Why?" As always he was caught up in her aura. The ethereal yet spirited, high-strung quality. One side of her gleaming hair fell forward in a thick inturned curve, the other was tucked very fetchingly behind her ear. She had changed her dress. This one some kind of gauzy slip, was the exact deep pink of the roses that grew in the garden.

"I don't want you to punish me like this."

His face was as boldly carved as a sculpture. "So what might compensate for all the pain you've delivered," he taunted. "Can I come to your room later? Peel off that dress? Could I wrap you around with my body, imprison you with my limbs? Could I make love to you until you're clinging to me, crying out to me to give you what you want?''

She felt her whole body go hot. ''You want a mistress not a wife,'' she said bitterly.

''In you I can get both. How long is it since we were together?''

She averted her head swiftly. ''I don't remember.''

''All right. I'll tell you.'' His laugh was soft and humourless. ''Six years, nine months and thirteen days. It's a hell of a long time to want a woman as much as I want you. It's like some relentless obsession. You'd think I'd finally be able to fling you off.''

It was so killingly new. This hostility. ''But you can't can you? Because you want Charlotte.''

''Of course. That's what it is. The days when our relationship was perfect are long gone.''

She blinked rapidly, fighting back tears, and he caught the point of her chin, seeped in a corrosive desire, pulses throbbing, possessed by her physical beauty.

The power of his kiss moved from her tongue and her lips to her throat. Drove deep into her breasts, right down to her stomach and the quivering area between her legs, cutting like a knife.

''Sleep with me.'' The words burst from him. ''I want you tonight.'' Now he gripped her body to his. Let her feel his sizzling desire.

''You despise me,'' she said fiercely. ''Do you think I can't read what goes on behind your eyes?''

''Why not? That's only one of your many skills. Swear you'll come to me or I'll come to you.'' His eyes glittered like black diamonds in his bronze face.

''I must have been mad to get into this situation,'' she agonised, seared by the thought.

"You *are* mad in my arms." He lifted his hand and grazed her flushed cheek.

"Call and I'll run?"

"Did I really say that?" he mocked.

"I hope not because I'm saying no! I have to reestablish myself, Nick, not lose myself in you."

So closely were they standing, so utterly intent on each other, they didn't hear Bebe's approach. Bebe, who'd had a sudden compulsion to check if everything was all right, stopped in confusion at the top of the stairs, one hand pressed to her heart. They hadn't been talking in whispers—she had caught some of the conversation and now she saw with her own eyes. Passion swirled around them so scorching Bebe actually felt its heat. For as long as she had known Nick he had never said a word about Suzannah, this woman so central to his past, so crucial to his future. Bebe wondered whatever could have happened, that they could confront each other in this manner. She found herself wishing with all her heart they could overcome the forces that had misshaped their lives. It was obvious to her now that both had been dealt some crushing blow to the psyche.

Later that night when the household had settled, Suzannah checked on Charley, settled the covers lovingly around her, then returned to the room that had been hers and Martin's, quietly turning the lock in the door. So overwhelming was her need for Nick she felt as much compelled to lock herself in as lock him out. She desperately wanted to go to him but knew she could not. All his feelings were in contradiction, like love and hate. She knew she would never win his trust again. No amount of passionate lovemaking could do that. One could never escape the past or its effects.

\*     \*     \*

In the morning she was up early, organising breakfast, a selection of juices, orange, grapefruit, pineapple, cereal for anyone who wanted it, luscious pawpaws and mangoes from North Queensland, to be followed by bacon, sausages and eggs with hash browns, toast, tea and coffee. She needed no help to prepare this first meal of the day but when she turned from slicing mangoes into a bowl, Nick, looking impossibly vibrant, entered the large kitchen.

"Sleep well?" he enquired so sardonically the blood rushed to her cheeks.

"Like a baby."

"That's why you have the softest shadows on your creamy skin. Can I help?"

"I believe I have everything under control."

"Well it's true you're a dab hand at orchestrating these things, but I didn't picture you in an apron."

"Sorry to shock you," she said coolly when the truth was it was the most wonderful thing to have him there with her.

"Can I set the table?" He put his arm around her and dropped a kiss on her head. "Where are we going to have it?"

His very touch was dizzying. "I thought the pavilion." She referred to an octagonal structure lined with French doors that led off into the garden. It had a marvellous contemporary glass chandelier poised low over a long glass-topped table that could seat a dozen people. Golden canes in huge green glazed pots created a fern-house atmosphere.

"What a good idea!" He sounded pleased. "I just love a woman with flair."

Suzannah ran her hands under the tap, dried them then

leaned back against the sink to face him. "How many women have you loved? Besides me?"

His eyes were jet-black. "Suzy, darling, you can't expect me to tell you about my affairs."

"Why? Is it so terribly hard?" she challenged.

The old spirit was back in her eyes but she looked as fragile as a lily. "You're the only constant in my life, Suzannah," he said. "I've had affairs, pleasant affairs to make life tolerable but nothing with a great deal of substance. I didn't for instance get *married*."

"Stop," she said. How could there be forgiveness when there was such bitterness?

"Some day soon, Suzannah, we have to talk this through," he told her, more harshly than he intended. "Didn't you realise you were pregnant with my child?"

"No," she lied, shaking her head when she remembered the very day. The day she had emptied out her stomach hiding away in the vineyards in sickness and panic. At least Mrs Konrads will know what to do, she had thought. She'll advise me, help me to find Nick.

"We can't turn the clock back, can we?" he said sombrely.

"It's very painful for me, too." She pushed on to another job.

"I know." He brought his hand to her cheek. "The answer is to get on with life."

"When you hate me?" Her voice almost broke.

"Hate you?" He took a long, slow breath. "Never. Despite everything I could never hate you, Suzannah. Death wouldn't change that."

Thirty minutes later the horde descended, everyone in high spirits, hungry for breakfast and eager to get out into the vineyards.

The townspeople arrived by nine o'clock, the women with picnic baskets containing additional goodies to add to the feast. It was going to be hot, hard, thirsty work but there was a beautiful, river-scented breeze blowing, a cacophony of birdsong, one wide sweep of white cloud chasing across a cobalt-blue sky. Charley sat cross-legged on the lawn with her cousins, all of them dressed in shorts and cotton shirts, sneakers on their feet, waiting patiently for directions.

Finally they were all off to create their instant vineyard, men, women and children, ready to dig, plant then fit up the new vines with guards like miniature greenhouses, before watering the vines in. It was a wonderful community turnout. As Suzannah did her bit, crouching low over the ploughed soil, calm returned and entered her soul. This was what caring for Mother Earth was all about. Eventually these vines would put forth berries in abundance producing wines of a distinctive and distinguished flavour. She was thrilled and gratified Nick, for all the intense pressures on him with his business, had taken on the responsibility of putting the Bellemont Farm vineyard and winery back on its feet. More, to make it grow and prosper. It was his German blood that made him love it all so much. German settlers, and the Schroeders were a prime example of this, were of major importance in the history of wine in Australia.

Everyone hastened down from the hills at midday to enjoy the lavish barbecue that had been prepared for so many dedicated workers. Great hopes were held for their efforts, the prospect of drinking wine from the vines they had planted. Many of the families who were there had members who had harvested Bellemont's grapes for fifty years and more. Marcus Sheffield had always paid his workers well but he had never put on a spread like this or encouraged such community participation. Nick Konrads's venture, clearly backed by Marcus Sheffield's daughter, generated immense goodwill. Even the local rural fire brigade was there with its water tanker. Pastoralists from all over the district, come to observe, found themselves happily helping out, caught up by the pervading sense of enthusiasm and achievement.

"I can't remember when I enjoyed myself more," Martin's sister Nicole said to Suzannah when the family was leaving, hugging her, her friendliness restoring the balance of their plummeting relationship.

It was a comment Suzannah and Nick were to hear many, many times over. If only this had happened before! But then, how could it? The formidable Marcus Sheffield had followed the very traditional path that established an unbridgeable gap between landowner and worker. All of that apparently was about to change. The town liked it.

As Suzannah and Nick stood waving people off the property, Frank Harris, the local police chief, dressed in a checked shirt and denim jeans, slid out of his private car and approached them. "Afternoon, Suzannah," he called. "Everyone seems to have had a whale of a day."

"Mr Konrads." He acknowledged Nick with respect. "I wondered if I might have a word with you?"

"May I ask about what?" Nick's tone was quiet but undeniably steely.

"Something I'd like to get off my chest." Frank Harris said in a straight voice. "I can say it in front of Suzannah here, if you want. But she's had too much laid on her for a long time."

"Mummy, Mummy," Charley called excitedly from the top of the steps. "Why don't we get the Christmas tree out? Bebe says it's December."

"I wouldn't think Bebe had any energy left,"

Suzannah laughed. "I'll be with you in a moment, darling." She turned back to Frank. "I'll leave you to have your talk, Frank. I hope Nancy is feeling better?" Nancy was his wife.

"Nothing an operation won't put right," Frank said, smiling bravely.

Some ten minutes later Suzannah heard Nick re-enter the house. "What was that all about?" she whispered, going to join him at the door.

His severe expression softened and his voice became gentle. "You sound like a little girl."

"I don't want anyone to hear," she said, holding up a finger to her lips.

Her eyes were a deep violet. Her expression sweet and concerned. He ached to say, "Suzannah, I love you. I love you with all my heart," but such an admission, amounting to a confession, required the right conditions and they never seemed to happen. Instead he took her hand, drawing her back onto the porch where they were out of earshot. "Guilt," he said with black humour. "Poor old Frank has been feeling guilt all these years."

"That's it?" She stared up at him, relief on her face.

He nodded. "He wanted my forgiveness for the part he played in running me out of town. He wasn't happy about it, he says. In fact the incident upset him for years. But your father was a very important man and he'd brought charges which Frank didn't properly allow me to defend. He cut the whole thing short. He turfed me out."

"That was terrible," Suzannah said.

"*You* listened to your father. Why not Frank?" He couldn't stop himself saying it.

"I truly didn't believe him, Nick. Not in my heart. So

what are you going to do now? I'm sure you could get Frank into a lot of trouble.''

''And how would that make me feel better?'' He looked at her questioningly. ''He's not a bad man. He buckled in to your father at the time. I understand his wife's condition is more serious than he's letting on.''

Suzannah was silent for a bit, nibbling on her lip. ''I must call in and see her. I spoke to her recently in town. She was her old cheerful self. To forgive Frank is an act of mercy, Nick.''

''Blessed are the merciful,'' he responded in a light, ironic tone. ''Frank's job is safe. But why didn't he have some guts at the time?''

''We both cried after you were gone, Nick,'' Suzannah said.

In the end everyone helped decorate the tree, Suzannah seizing Charley every now and again to hug her, her joy was so infectious.

They used all the ornaments of Christmas. Balls and baubles in rich Christmas colours of scarlet, emerald, silver and gold, sparkling tinsel winding around the pendulous branches, coloured lights to cast a bright glow, fastened into position by Nick. At the very top was the Star of Bethlehem, symbol of peace, a beautiful ornament that had been in the Sheffield family for many many years, its surface encrusted with Austrian crystals that glittered like diamonds.

''All we need now is presents,'' Charley said, clasping Nick's hand and looking up cajolingly into his face. ''You will come back, won't you, Nick? You will come back for Christmas.''

Bebe wasn't the only one to witness the love that flashed into his eyes, stayed there shimmering, spreading over the child.

"Lord, will you look at that!" Bebe whispered to Noel Geddes, who stood beside her holding her hand.

"Oh yes, he loves the child," Noel murmured back. He knew his former pupil very well.

# CHAPTER SEVEN

IT WAS quiet after everyone had left, Bebe electing to travel with Noel in his Land Cruiser.

"Thank you so much for a wonderful weekend, Suzannah," Bebe said as she was leaving, moving forward to kiss Suzannah's cheek. "Nick desperately needs some private time for relaxation. This place is a miracle. He works so hard."

"I'm going to call in sick tomorrow," Nick joked. "If you're going back with Noel, I think I'll drive back tomorrow."

Suzannah didn't hear the rest for the sound of her blood roaring in her ears. She and Nick alone in the house together! After such a weekend of activity six-year-old Charley would go off to bed early, sleeping the fathoms deep sleep of the innocent. What would everyone think? She had tried to imagine the private conversations over the weekend though no one, most of all Bebe, seemed to find it odd she and Charley were living in Nick's new country house. So she was the daughter of the former owner? So her family had worked Bellemont Farm for generations? She had anticipated a few privately raised eyebrows. But that had been far from the case. Everyone seemed to accept her as Nick's dearest, closest friend who had suffered two bereavements. Her husband, then her father. It was too much to cope with alone.

Then again, Suzannah reasoned, it must be because Nick's friends, the people who worked for him, overtly worshipped him. If they were to be believed, the world

was a different place for them because of Nick. He inspired them, he had faith in them, in their abilities, let
them run with them, recompensed them marvellously for
the effort they put in. Konrads was a team. Nick treated
his staff as equals but they all knew his brain power was
vastly superior. It was quite wonderful the way he had
no side to him, one of the young women told her. Nick
was interested in everyone and what they were doing.
Suzannah listened to a lot of words of praise about Nick.
The townspeople, once they got over the shock of his
return and the news that he had bought Bellemont, recognised him as one of them again. Many of the women,
now married, remembered they had been in love with him
right through high school and wrung their hands he had
never looked in their direction. Most were fairly certain
Marcus Sheffield had applied a lot of emotional blackmail to get Suzannah to marry Martin White. It was almost like a novel with people's actions defying reason.

Charley, of course, was ecstatic Nick was staying, insisting her mother brush her hair so Nick could see how
nice it was out of her plaits.

"I imagine you as a beautiful young woman," Nick
told her, sitting in an armchair, watching his daughter
turn slowly so he could see that the tips of her hair almost
reached her waist. As Charley was growing so was her
hair in glossy abundance. He remembered his mother's
lovely hair, as polished as a black cockatoo's wing.
Startled he realised Charley's hairline was becoming
more pronounced. He stared at her in her pretty pink
dress, a muscle along his jawline working, as he recognised his daughter had inherited not only her grandmother's eyes but his distinctive widow's peak. It wasn't
something a lot of people had. How many others had
noticed it as well? The truth would hurt a lot of people.

Over his daughter's gleaming head he met Suzannah's eyes, reading in them a reflection of his own thoughts.

"Come on, Nick, talk to me," Charley suddenly said. "Why are you looking at Mummy like that? Staring so deep into her."

"I was thinking how much you're like her, Charlotte," Nick said, getting up and holding out his hand. "Why don't we take a little stroll before it gets dark. We can see how Gypsy and Lady are. Early in the New Year the horses will arrive. Your mother and I are going to pick them out. I expect you'd like to come along, too?"

"Really? You're serious?" Charley danced beside him.

"I know when I'm in the presence of a horsewoman." Nick looked down at her and smiled.

After the delicious lunch Suzannah prepared to speed Nick's guests on their way, they settled for a light tea of scrambled eggs and smoked salmon with fingers of toast. It was one of Charley's favourite meals and she ate it with relish.

"Shall I say my prayers now and get them over?" she asked her mother as Nick went off to check the house and mother and daughter began to clear away.

"Why the hurry, darling?" Suzannah asked.

"Nick has promised to tell me a bedtime story. It's a ghost story, I think."

"Can't be," Suzannah said. "You have far too much imagination already."

"But it's a lovely story, Nick said. His mother used to tell it to him when he was a little boy. It's about Christmas."

"Ah, I see. Then we must trust Nick, mustn't we?"

Charley followed her mother into the kitchen, set down

some plates, then asked, "Do you love him, Mummy, as a friend?" It was obvious she had been pondering their relationship.

Suzannah's heart jumped. "Yes, I do, darling. I've known Nick since I was a little girl. I told you."

"Wasn't he your Prince Charming?" Charley stared up at her as though she had figured it out.

"Why ever would you say that?" The blood rushed into Suzannah's cheek and she turned away quickly to stack the dishwasher.

"When you look at him you look like you're daydreaming." Charley came closer and peered at her.

"I'll be darned," Suzannah laughed. "How can you tell when someone is daydreaming?"

"Easy. They get this faraway look on their face. Nick said you used to go every day to visit his mother. He said his mother taught you to play the piano."

"Darling, I always told you Mrs Konrads taught me to play." Suzannah stooped to load the dinner plates.

"I didn't know who Mrs Konrads was," Charley explained. "I didn't know she was Nick's mother. I'd like to see the house they lived in. Nick told me his mother went to join his father in Heaven where they're both perfectly happy."

Suzannah stopped what she was doing to stroke her daughter's cheek. "I should think they would be. They were very good people."

"Who were?" Nick asked, thinking he could have been blessed with this sight for years. His wife and his daughter. Suzannah had a very special way with their child.

"Charley was saying she would like to see where your parents lived."

"We have a little problem there, Charlotte," Nick replied, "no one lives there any more."

"Is it haunted?" Charley gave a little shiver.

"Every old house has a past, Charlotte. Just like this one. Good people leave a good atmosphere."

Charley moved closer and leaned against him endearingly. "I'd really like to see where you grew up. I'd like to see where Mummy had her music lessons. I'd like to stand on the verandah where Mrs Konrads used to wave her goodbye." She focused her beautiful eyes on Nick's face. "What were your parents' names?"

Over Charley's head their yes met. Emotions passed without words. "My mother's name was Lotte," Nick told his daughter simply. "My father's name was Carl. That's the German form of Charles. Both of them were wonderful people, wonderful looking, too."

"They must have been!" Charley sounded absolutely certain. "You're so *handsome*. My cousins think so, too. Weren't your parents Australians? You've got a little accent."

"Most people place it." He smiled. "New Australians they were called in those days, Charlotte. People from many lands came to settle in Australia...the United Kingdom, all over Europe, South-East Asia. We're what is known as a multicultural society much like the United States."

"Yes, I know. We learn that at school." Charley's small face flushed with pride. "Some of the kids in the class speak *two* languages. Aren't they lucky?"

"Maybe we'd better start you on a couple," Nick suggested. "French and German."

"You'll have to do it, Nick," Suzannah said quietly. "You're infinitely more qualified than I am."

"You just need to travel a bit more," he said with a long look.

"Will you, Nick?" Charley piped up.

He bent and lifted her into his arms. "Sweetie, that's a promise."

"I knew it would be," Charley said. "Bebe told me you're the best!"

It was another hour before Charley was settled in her bed, listening enthralled to Nick's Christmas story. She hadn't heard such a good story in years, not even Mummy's. This was a little bit spooky, but good spooky, leaving her with a magical feeling. She hugged Jacko, the clown she still took to bed with her, her eyelids drooping deliciously by the time Nick got to the end of his wonderfully exciting story.

"That was great, Nick!" She felt for his hand resting on the coverlet and squeezed with her little girl strength. "I love stories about forests and medieval castles. I even love the Brothers Grimm. Sometimes they're really scary. I think I'll go to sleep now."

"Sweet dreams, *meine liebling*," he said, his voice conveying the profound tenderness he felt.

Immediately Charley's long lashes came flying open. "I haven't heard *that* before," she said in wonderment. "I haven't heard you speak like that with a *real* accent. What does it mean, *miner leebling?*"

Suzannah, who had come to stand very quietly at the bedroom door, found her throat working. She put her hand to it, fighting down tears. How had she possibly kept from Nick the fact he had a daughter? A daughter who loved him from the first sight. Instinctively. A daughter who would bring back images of his own mother every time he looked at her. She felt unbearably moved, unbearably saddened.

Nick was replying, his voice so vibrant, so loving, it invaded the caverns of her heart. "It means little sweetheart, Charlotte."

"Oh, I wish I was *your* sweetheart," Charley said fervently.

"But you are," her father replied. "You *are*."

This time Charley's eyelids fell. A smile on her face, she turned on her side, curled up, two hands beneath her cheek, the signal she was off to dreamland.

Nick, oblivious of Suzannah's presence, bent to kiss her temple, standing for a moment staring down at his sleeping daughter before he turned off the lights. No plunging into instant darkness; subdued lighting was always left on in the hallway as a comfort for family and guests.

Before Suzannah had time to recover, unable to wipe the poignant expression from her face, Nick turned to see her framed in the doorway utterly exposed, sadness naked in her eyes, pleading in their depths. His need for her was boundless no matter how much she had made him suffer. He was bound to her irrevocably. Bound to her and their daughter. She had one hand resting against the doorframe as if she were using it for support. He couldn't be sure but were there tracks of tears on her lovely face? The anger vanished. The hunger remained.

"Suzannah!" he murmured, his arms going out to her without his volition. He moved towards her, the light on the pearly cleft of her breasts as the neckline of her dress pushed low. A cool ripple of silk met his fingers, warming instantly to his touch. He cupped his hands, letting them fold over the delicate contours, feeling her nipples spring into tight buds. He could smell her own unique fragrance, clean and light, like a breath of air in the citrus grove. "You're crying."

Now he could clearly see the sheen of tears. He bent forward irresistibly, tongue curling, to take a crystal droplet into his mouth. Her eyes were half shut. She was breathing fast.

"Suzannah," he said again, hands on her shoulders moving her away from the bedroom into the hallway.

Whatever she read in his eyes she fled from him blindly, covering the distance to the staircase like a winged nymph. What a wonderful flight she had, swift and springy. He went after her purposefully as she knew he would, his heart thrashing passionately, emotion thick and dangerous in the air.

She ran straight to the library, large, rich, opulent, books from floor to ceiling, flinging herself into her father's favourite chair. Not a chair, a Gothic *throne,* mammoth in its size. Her eyes were nearly purple with intensity, her hair flowing around her creamy, pointed face. Almost directly behind her over the mantel her father's portrait was back in place. Marcus Sheffield, lord of the manor, in his prime. Six foot two, broad chested, impressive in his tweeds, his handsome head capped by a full head of steel-grey hair.

"Back to your father, eh?" he rasped, all of his senses burning. "Back to Daddy's protection. He'll take care of you." Anger flared around him like lightning in a great storm.

"He's not here to take care of me any more," she wept as if heartbroken, small and fragile in that wretched chair.

"You think I'm going to rape you?" He was incredibly, furiously outraged, his nerves live wires.

She let her head fall back against the high carved back, sobbing quietly for her sins, sobbing for the weakness she had shown when she should have shown strength. "I have to make sure...I have to make sure..." The words tumbled into one another.

"Sure of what?" He advanced on her, infuriated bewilderment stamped in every plane and angle of his face. "That you won't fall pregnant. *Again?*"

She recoiled. "Sure that you *love* me." She watched him looming over her, scorched by his glance. "I don't want to be just a *prize,* Nick," she pleaded. "Something you've hard won. Like Bellemont. I'll gladly share Charlotte with you."

The very air had gone electric. "Will you tell her I'm her father?" he demanded, holding her eyes with such force she at last averted her head.

"That's between you and me."

"You must think people are fools," he laughed, intolerant of her answer. "Charlotte will grow more and more like me as she gets older."

"God, it's happening now." She brushed furiously at her tears with the heel of her hand.

"Get out of that chair," he said.

"You can't make me."

The moment stretched to breaking point. "I could easily, Suzannah, but don't let that happen. We need to be civilised for our child."

"But you'd make me marry you?"

His eyes caught fire. "You're a woman to die for."

The bitter irony was insupportable. "Yes, I know." Her voice held an agony of regret. "I didn't make poor Martin happy."

"You should never have married him," he retaliated, "or did you think you'd have a fighting chance?"

The full realisation of what she had done to him hit her with great force. "All right, Nick, I made a total mess of things. I wasn't thinking very clearly at the time. I was so full of panic and grief.''

His handsome features were taut with emotion. "Because you knew you were pregnant to me. God, are you so bloody neurotic you have to deny it?''

"You went away." She bowed her head, her eyelashes like black feathery wings against her pale cheeks. "After that my whole life was derailed.''

This he knew all about. He moved agitatedly away from her, determined the portrait of Marcus Sheffield would come down from the library. How blind that man had been. Such a colossal ego sacrificing his own daughter. The daughter he adored. It made no sense. "Would you *ever* have tried to contact me again?" His voice was quieter, but he couldn't hold back the anger. "Would you ever have let me know I had a daughter or were you content to live a lie? To start up again with someone else your father hand-picked?''

They might have been absolutely isolated. The only two people left in the world.

Her own anger ignited from his. "What would you have had me do? Plunge back into a love that has dominated my life? Do you know what it's like to sleep with someone night after night, year in and year out, and ache for someone else?" A long-damned current burst out of her. "That's what it was like for me...I felt exploited. Martin thought he could win through in the end, win control, and he didn't care how he did it. It didn't happen, and God, the loneliness!''

An exquisite spear of pain cut into him. "Don't you understand, Suzannah, you did it all?''

"Am I going to have to pay forever?" She leapt to her feet, intent on rushing past him but he pulled her to him with a furious curse.

"Do you want to see *my* scars? Do you?"

"Damn you, Nick." She flinched when she was filled with the most incredible liquefying desire. "I can't take any more." Her whole body felt hot and heavy, full of the aches of a frustrated passion that rose from her very core.

"Give yourself to me," he said in a low, bewitching voice.

She thought she would curl up in flames.

"Suzannah!"

She couldn't trust her voice, only the primal intelligence of her body that was pressing forward to fuse with his.

"I can't move." She gave the ghost of a little moan.

"Don't think about it. I'll carry you."

It was absurdly easy for him to lift her off the ground, and carry her along the softly lit corridor to the haven of her room.

The same room where Charlotte had been given the gift of life.

He put her down on the bed where she lay arms outstretched, one trailing gracefully to the carpeted floor. "I want to undress you." His voice was infinitely moving, no longer harsh and angry.

"Kiss me," she begged, without the defences she had learned over the years. This was Nick, the person who with their daughter meant more to her than anyone else in the world.

He bent over her, his striking face deeply passionate, visibly affected by her beauty and her infinitely tender expression. This was *his* Suzannah before all the terrible things had happened to them. He pressed his mouth down over hers, feeling the soft cushions of her lips part for him so he could slide his tongue over hers and move

deeper into the sweet, moist cavity. His heart was rapping
hard against his ribs, flesh tautening, tightening, expanding, taking the dominant role. How could anyone pervert
their love? She was sighing gently beneath his hands,
moving her slender body accommodatingly so he could
strip the slip of a dress from her. How many times over
the past years had he imagined this? Sometimes his
dreams of her had continued right through the night. Until
dawn. His body contorted with sexual frustration and the
pain of loss.

His accelerated heartbeat thundered in his ears like
breakers on the shore. Finally her naked body was bathed
in the rose glow from the bedside lamps and he sat completely still staring at her as if she was his very own
creation, the same luminous skin, the same girlish frame,
delicate shoulders, breasts small and high, waist narrow,
long feather-light limbs, the slight curve of her stomach.
Childbirth hadn't changed her at all, the years Martin
White had bent over her beautiful body. The thought
coming as it did almost tore him apart, his hardened features incapable of veiling it.

"I'm so sorry, so sorry." She looked up at him with
her wonderful violet eyes, pulses fluttering at her throat
and her temples.

He stood up so violently he sent some ornament flying.
She was all around him and he couldn't hold his hunger
to check. It was like a blinding flame, a furnace, a force
field, whatever you wanted to call it and it was exerting
its full power. On him. On her. He could see the coursing
blood flushing her body. He could see her fearful elation.

He began stripping off his own clothes in a long streak
of ecstasy, his nostrils flaring, as he imagined finding the

furthest reaches of her. Places no one had gone but him.
Tonight he would obliterate all memories of the past from
her mind. He was back to claim his woman. And his
child.

# CHAPTER EIGHT

THERE was a new feeling about Bellemont Farm that infected everybody. The word had gone out far and wide that the vineyards were going to be bigger and better than ever before. Experts had been called in to advise on the best location for a new cellar and tradesmen from the town descended on the estate in force to begin on a long list of repairs.

Never again will I have to defer to my father or to Martin, Suzannah thought. Nick might own everything but there was no struggle between them for ascendancy, rather a shared strategy. Their minds had always worked on the same plane. Nick trusted her to do what she knew best. She had been part of this for so long she knew exactly what she had to do to make Bellemont thrive now that she was given free rein.

All the workers on the estate became used to seeing her walking through the vineyards making her daily inspections. Alone or accompanied by either Hans or Kurt Schroeder. Often she stopped to have a chat with a worker in the field or she was found in the low-vaulted passages of the wine cellar given over to the storage of the Chardonnay with its clean, delicate character. Nick was keen on developing the Rhine Riesling, which Suzannah preferred to the Chardonnay, her father's commercial choice. Negotiations were already going on to acquire Sevenhill Farm on their western boundary. A property of about eighty hectares with a family tradition of making dessert wines. Production had dwindled since

the owner had lost his two sons to the attractions of city life.

The riding school, too, preoccupied her mind. The school was to offer riding tuition, dressage, show jumping, cross country. Of the people Suzannah had interviewed, Nick had given her the okay to select three of the applicants, two well-qualified women and right out of the blue a young man she had known for years, a brilliant rider, who had been selected for the forthcoming Olympic team. When Nick could find the time they intended to visit several studs to buy experienced horses for Bellemont. Ex-racehorses, show horses for the advanced riders, quiet, sensible horses for the children. Shetland ponies could sometimes be irritable, Arabs too temperamental for children to control. She well remembered her father taking her up before him long before he bought her her first pony, a darling Connemara called Sunrise when she was quite a bit younger than Charley. She had won dozens of ribbons as a schoolgirl and she prided herself on the skills imparted to her by her highly accredited coach, long retired.

Suzannah was talking to the foreman responsible for getting the olympic-size indoor arena back to its top condition—Bellemont Farm had prided itself on its magnificent facilities—when Hans called to her.

"You have a visitor, Suzannah. She's waiting for you on the porch."

"Did she give her name, Hans?" Suzannah asked cautiously, walking out into the radiant sunlight. She wasn't expecting anyone.

"She said only you knew her." Hans shrugged.

Why then the panic?

"What does she look like?" Suzannah walked with Hans across the cobbled courtyard.

"I hope I did right, Suzannah?" Hans, catching something tentative in her manner, looked dismayed.

"Of course you did." Suzannah patted his arm. "It's just that I wasn't expecting anyone."

"To be honest—" Hans scratched his ear "—I've never seen her before. But she's very respectable, all right. A good-looking woman driving a BMW."

"Bright chestnut hair?" Suzannah very nearly gasped.

Now Hans was looking agitated. "Like a new penny. If you want, Suzy, I can get rid of her."

Suzannah laughed a little grimly. "I'd better take care of it, Hans. You can stay close. I'm sure I'll have to tell her to go."

"You mean she's trouble?" Hans didn't want anyone causing Suzannah trouble. He had known her since she was a baby. He understood the sufferings in her life.

"I can't imagine what else it would be." Suzannah tried to ease her expression. "Don't worry, Hans. I'll take care of it."

"And I'll be in the rose garden giving Archie a hand. Just in case."

"Thank you, Hans." Suzannah knew perfectly well she could trust Hans with her life.

The woman called Adrienne was sitting calmly on the porch looking up with a pleasant smile when she saw Suzannah approaching.

"Good morning," she called. "I was passing and I knew I just had to come in and see you."

"If you don't mind, I have a problem with that," Suzannah said coolly, walking up the short flight of steps. "Nick never did say, but I'm certain you were the person who sent the poison-pen letter to my late father."

The woman looked at her as if she'd gone mad. "Please allow me to express my sympathy," she said.

"It broke my heart when I lost my own father. He was very dear to me." She stood up, advancing towards Suzannah, hand out. "We haven't met properly, I know. I'm Adrienne Alleman. I'm a good friend of Nick's."

Suzannah ignored her outstretched hand.

"I'm sorry, Miss or is it Mrs Alleman?"

"Mrs Alleman," Adrienne supplied, letting her hand drop with a mock wry expression. "I'm a widow like yourself." Her cat's eyes narrowed over Suzannah's face and body. "I must say you're very beautiful. Even in a T-shirt and jeans. I can quite see how Nick got himself so very involved with you."

"Perhaps you could tell me, Mrs Alleman, exactly why you're here?" Suzannah asked crisply.

"May I sit down?" Adrienne raised her delicate winged brows as if finding Suzannah's social skills wanting.

"For a short time, certainly." Suzannah took the wicker chair opposite her.

"How extraordinary it is to be talking to you," Adrienne mused. "I've had so many run-throughs in my head."

"I can quite believe it," Suzannah responded. "Forgive me, but I'm viewing you as the enemy here. You didn't deny sending that letter to my father?"

"What would be the point? You've convicted me already." Adrienne brushed a nonexistent speck off her short jade linen shirt. "Though I can't deny we women have a great capacity for vengeance."

"I shy away from it myself," Suzannah said coldly.

"Ah, then I have a good, strong, positive nature." Adrienne's tone turned quite spiteful. "You know the old adage, all's fair in love and war."

"How did it help *you?*" Suzannah asked. "Nick was

filled with dismay and disgust at your actions. He doesn't operate that way and he doesn't have any time for people who do.''

"He loved me once.'' Adrienne's face twisted, calling forth a pang of pity.

"Did he tell you that?'' Suzannah asked more gently.

"Every time we made love,'' Adrienne said and threw up her head. "I couldn't count the number of times. He's a wonderful lover, isn't he? So passionate and imaginative. He knows exactly when you like it a bit rough, the wonderful moments to be tender.'' The quaver in her voice belied her challenging demeanour.

"I'm sorry if you've been hurt,'' Suzannah murmured, pained by visions of Nick and this woman together. No wonder Nick hated any thought of Martin.

"Sorry isn't good enough, my dear,'' Adrienne answered. "No need to look at me with your purple eyes and *don't* play the nun. I was devastated when I found out Nick had fathered your child. He never said a word.''

"For the simple reason he didn't know,'' Suzannah responded, watching Adrienne frown disapprovingly.

"You mean you kept it a secret from him?'' Adrienne shook her head in horror. "And you have the hide to question me?''

"I didn't realise I was answerable to you, Mrs Allemen,'' Suzannah said coldly. "You play no part in my life. As I understand it you no longer play a part in Nick's.''

Adrienne laughed. "Well of course you expect me to give him up gracefully. Terribly sweet idea, but it's not on. Nick led me to believe we would marry. He allowed me to fall deeply in love with him. Now he expects me to get lost because his darling Suzannah is back on the market. How convenient for you both your husband was killed.''

Suzannah wasn't about to sit around and be insulted. ''You didn't know my husband so don't talk about him, Mrs Alleman.''

Adrienne gave her a pinched smile. ''My contacts tell me he had a young woman in the car with him.''

''Who died as well,'' Suzannah pointed out grimly. ''She was very young. I refuse to talk about it.''

''What about we discuss the subject of your child?'' Adrienne challenged. ''Nick's child. I know, too, the White family believe her to be one of them. It's said her grandmother, her aunts and her cousins adore her.''

All at once Suzannah felt ill. ''What are you getting at?'' she demanded.

''A deal.'' Adrienne leaned towards her as if they were friends. ''Invent some scenario to send Nick off. You're very good at it, I believe. Do that and I won't be sending off any more letters.''

''You'd write to Martin's mother?'' Suzannah looked at her with contempt.

''I think I have a legitimate reason.'' Adrienne raised her arched brows. ''You're the deceitful one of the two of us.''

When horrors hit, they hit hard. ''You can't possibly think such an action would endear you to Nick?'' Suzannah asked.

''Oh, I know he'll retaliate if he finds out,'' the older woman shrugged. ''He could very likely ruin me in business if he chose, but I've always looked on him as a compassionate man. Until *now*.''

''You're wrong to think I'd keep it from him.'' Suzannah threw down the gauntlet.

"What exactly are your plans?" Adrienne asked angrily.

"Nick and I will be getting married after a period of mourning for my father."

"You surely can't be thinking of getting married in this town?" Adrienne sneered in disbelief.

"It's none of your business."

"I think I warned you. I'm going to make it my business," Adrienne snorted. "Maybe Nick will never come back to me but he sure as hell is not going to forget me."

God, she's got eyes like a falcon, Suzannah thought. "Just how much are you capable of?" she asked.

Adrienne laughed dangerously. "I'll stop short of murder. Only because I'd very likely be caught. I never quite realised how powerful is my jealous streak. But then I've never met anyone remotely like Nick in my life. I believe I'd still have a chance if only you would bow out."

Suzannah shook her head. "That's not going to happen. Nick has set his whole mind to our getting married. Nothing I could do would dissuade him. Not now. Not ever. You mustn't know Nick as well as you think you do."

Adrienne stood up, pushing back her wicker chair. "Then it seems I have to do your job for you. Let Mrs White know the child she's adored all these years is no relation at all. If it's true you and Nick are going to get married, then I'm dead-set on spoiling things for you. People don't talk about 'a woman scorned' for nothing. Nick cheated on me. There's not going to be a happy ending."

The morning hadn't been heralded by any ill omens, Suzannah thought later. Everything had started out so well. She had dropped Charley off to play with her cousins, observing how Valerie, Martin's mother, stood waving her off, an arm around each grandchild, Charley and Laura, with Lucy playing with the family collie dog, trying unsuccessfully to make it fetch a ball. It was a scene she had witnessed many times, grateful for the family togetherness, but since Martin's death and Nick's reappearance in her life it had all become very sad and confronting. The very last thing she wanted to do was inflict more pain but since Adrienne Alleman's visit it struck her she didn't have much option. It would be terrible for Martin's mother to find out Charley wasn't her grandchild under any circumstances but to receive a letter from a vindictive stranger! All that remained was for Suzannah to find the strength to make her confession. That very afternoon when she picked Charley up. Nick would be ringing in the evening and she would have to think carefully what to say to him. What residual feeling did he have for Adrienne? He had cared for her once. Their affair must have gone a long way for Adrienne to believe it would culminate in marriage. Adrienne Alleman was a striking-looking woman who would turn heads, but she had been given a great handicap in life. She had no compassion.

Around three-thirty that afternoon Suzannah drove the dozen kilometres to the White riverfront estate with its gracious elegance and lushly landscaped gardens. Like Bellemont the plantation-style homestead was regarded as one of the finest residences in the State. She and Martin had grown up very much the rich kids of the district, neither of them thinking very much about it, the beauty and tranquillity of their surroundings, having pretty much everything they wanted. It was just the way it *was*, one of the bonds they shared. Nick was the catalyst that changed their lives. She supposed had there been no Nick, Martin might well have kept his easygoing charm instead of having it destroyed by the jealousy that ran deep in his veins. She had certainly been fond of him. She might even have come to marry him freely only Nick had stolen her heart when she was just a child. As she had stolen his in equal measure.

Martha, the housekeeper, greeted her warmly, showing her through the house to the rear garden with its turquoise swimming pool and cabana. Valerie was relaxing on a recliner, feet from the three little girls sporting happily in the sparkling water. All three raised their hands, calling out a welcome. Martha sat upright, a warm smile on her gracious face.

"Ah, Suzy, I was just planning some afternoon tea. Have you time to join us?"

It was now or never. She could no longer shield anyone from the truth. It would inevitably come out as she had always known. "Actually, Valerie," she said, unaware her face was very pale, "I must speak to you privately." Valerie looked so at ease Suzannah deeply regretted the need to upset her, but Adrienne's visit weighed heavily on her.

Her mother-in-law didn't look entirely surprised. "Certainly, dear. Let's get the girls out of the pool. They can get changed and Martha can give them their afternoon tea in the conservatory."

"I've had such fun, Mummy," Charley exclaimed, coming up to Suzannah and accepting the towel her mother was holding out to her. "Laura and Lucy are dying to enrol in our riding school."

"That's lovely." Suzannah smiled at the two pretty little girls, Nicole's children, blond-haired, blue-eyed, as all the White offspring tended to be.

"Grandma said you'd pick out our ponies, Aunty Suzy." Lucy looked up to her, eyes bright with pleasure.

"Leave it to me." Suzannah reached out and patted the child's cheek in the affectionate way that drew people to her. "You'll have to start thinking up names."

There was a lot of excited chatter in the cabana as the girls changed back into their summer outfits of cool cotton tops and shorts.

"What about Prince?"

"What about Blaze?"

"I like Misty." Ponies names were flashed back and forth.

Finally Martha came out to collect them while Suzannah and Valerie had their talk.

"Shall we walk in the garden?" Valerie invited, taking Suzannah's arm. "You can tell me what you think of my latest idea. A couple of ponds near the temple house. Possibly a weir dividing them?"

"Sounds lovely." Suzannah mentally visualised the effect. "Another water garden would act as a gentle contrast to the drama of the temple."

"Just what I thought," Valerie said, pleased. "Now what is it that's troubling your mind, Suzannah? You're so pale, dear. It hasn't been an easy time for any of us."

"All the more reason why I don't want to upset you further." The distress was very evident in Suzannah's voice.

Valerie looked off at the beautiful vista of her garden, at the marvel of the summer flowering. "We're very close, aren't we, Suzy?" she asked.

Suzannah hugged her mother-in-law's arm. "I love you, Valerie. You know that. But I've been living a lie for which I blame myself profoundly. It can't go on any more."

"Why don't you just tell me?" Valerie said. They had reached a stone garden seat and both moved to sit down.

Suzannah turned a poignant face to her mother-in-law. "Valerie..." She hesitated a moment, feeling terrible then plunged on, "I must tell you before another day goes by, Charlotte isn't—"

"Martin's child?" Valerie broke in, her voice gentle, but emphatic. "Why do you choose to tell me now?"

It was like a moment of utter stillness after an explosion. "Did you hear what I just said, Valerie?" Suzannah pleaded. "You don't sound shocked. Or even surprised."

Valerie nodded her white-gold head. "What's so shocking about it, my dear? I think I've always known. Certainly long before it occurred to Martin."

"And you never said anything?" Suzannah stared at her, biting into her bottom lip.

Valerie's tone was level. I was never *exactly* sure. Besides, I'd grown to love our little Charley. There's something so utterly sweet about her. Utterly special. I could never hurt her. You see how the children are together. They're family."

"What am I to do?" Suzannah asked forlornly.

"Face the truth," Valerie said. "She's Nick child, of course."

Suzannah bowed her head. "Yes. I never dared to tell him."

The breeze was warm but Valerie gave a little shiver. "I have a clear picture of his mother in my head. I only met her a few times in the town. She was very quiet, very reserved but obviously refined. She had a very memorable face. Very memorable eyes. Charley's eyes."

Suzannah looked at her. "I don't expect you to forgive me, Valerie."

"There's a certain peace in having it out," Valerie said

and patted Suzannah's arm comfortingly. "It's your father I can't forgive," Valerie said. "Maybe in a way my own hopes put a lot of pressure on you. It was my dream you and Martin would marry one day. Maybe it would even have happened the way I wanted, only Nick Konrads came along. I don't blame you, Suzannah, for loving him. He was, *is,* quite remarkable. Dazzling really. I gather he didn't know about Charlotte until just recently?"

Suzannah nodded. "I fully intended to honour my marriage, Valerie. There was a price to pay."

"Even when your father and Martin manipulated the whole situation for their own ends?" Valerie asked, looking into Suzannah's eyes. "Martin felt terribly sorry about it later on. He confided to me his part in getting Nick Konrads banished from town. Make no mistakes, your father fully intended an innocent young man go to jail if he didn't accept his ultimatum.

"I don't want to speak ill of your father, Suzannah, I know how much you loved him, but you must have been aware he was in his way a benevolent despot. 'A control freak' Martin used to call him. He couldn't continue to control you, the one person he loved, if you married a dynamic young man like Nick Konrads. It was a darn sight easier with my poor Martin. Martin lacked strength. He became your father's man right before my eyes. Had his own father lived things might have been different. As it was!" Valerie shook her head.

"It's all so sad," Suzannah said, her heart constricting momentarily in her chest.

"And we must put it behind us," Valerie maintained firmly. There was nothing cold, or punishing or revengeful about her. "This can't be kept a private matter, can it, Suzannah?" she asked. "A man like Nick Konrads would want to claim his child. Of course you should have married him. I never did understand.''

Suzannah began to cry and Valerie put her arm around her. ''Mrs Konrads refused to tell me where he was,'' Suzannah explained, fighting for control. ''I had caused Nick enough pain. I didn't tell her I was pregnant. The 'fear' in her attitude stopped me. I think it had something to do with their old life in Europe. When they became refugees. I was young. I'd led such a sheltered life. I suppose if I dare admit it I was in awe of my father. He was very sharp with me at that time. He kept insisting Nick was not a man to be trusted. I was sick for a while. I couldn't cope.''

''That was how he compelled you and Martin to get married. I was thrilled and delighted at the time but later I began to see how it was. I know how much you tried to make your marriage work, Suzannah, but Martin developed a sense of hopelessness about him. He loved you but as much as you tried you could never love him. Not in the way he wanted. The way you love Nick Konrads.''

On the way home in the car Charley kept looking at her mother very carefully. ''What were you and Nanna talking about?'' she asked finally with an expression of anxiety.

''Family matters, darling,'' Suzannah said, urging herself to smile.

''I didn't think anything about the family would make you cry?'' Charley said doubtfully.

Thank God Valerie loved Charley unconditionally, Suzannah thought. Thank God for women like Valerie. She mightn't be that fortunate with the rest of the family.

''We were talking about...Daddy, sweetheart,'' she explained.

"Do you miss him terribly, Mummy?" Charley asked, unsure of the whole relationship.

"He wasn't only my husband, darling." Suzannah glanced at her reassuringly. "I knew him all my life. I was as close to Martin and his sisters as you are to Lucy and Laura."

Charley flushed. "I don't think Daddy loved me," Charley said.

It was stunning how much this child knew. "We've discussed this before, my love. Martin had a problem with expressing his feelings." Already he was Martin. Not "Daddy".

"He loved *you*, though," Charley said, very directly. "Maybe he didn't have enough love to go around. He didn't care I did so well at school. He didn't care they put me up a grade. He didn't care I'm really good at the piano or I love and understand horses. Why can I look at Nick and love him when I didn't feel like that with Daddy?"

Perhaps because he's your real father, Suzannah thought. But how and when am I going to tell you. She was convinced Adrienne Alleman would stick to her vindictive plan. She had asked Valerie to destroy the letter on sight. "It's very easy to love Nick," was all Suzannah said.

He rang that night, trembling a little when Suzannah told him of Adrienne's visit and what Adrienne planned to do. "She's determined to 'spoil things', Nick. Her own words."

"I promise you she won't do that." His tone was a mixture of anger and determination.

"In any case, I told Martin's mother." Suzannah held the phone tightly.

"Good God!" His expelled breath shivered down the wires. "Couldn't you have rung me before you decided what to do, Suzannah? We should have discussed this, the far-reaching consequences, the difficulties for Charlotte let alone anyone else."

"Valerie knew," she told him quietly. "She said she had always felt it but her love for Charley remains unchanged."

Nick didn't answer for a moment. "She must be a good woman."

"She is," Suzannah sighed. "Her reaction took a terrible weight from my shoulders."

"You've had a very upsetting day." His voice was inflected with a deep understanding.

"Telling Valerie was the hard part," she said. "I rather enjoyed telling Mrs Alleman to get the hell off the property. I thought it was still mine."

"How badly do you want it?" he asked, sounding strange.

"What does that mean, Nick?" She grappled to understand it.

"Work it out," he replied. "Love for a house can be more durable than love for a man."

"Is this a riddle?" She had an uncertain, lost sensation.

"I used to think not, now I'm not so sure. Bellemont is very important to you."

"So are *you,* Nick," she hastened to add. She desperately wished to see his face. Feel his arms around her again.

Silence persisted for a moment, then he said, "I'm no good at coming second, Suzannah. I want *all* of you. Only fair when I've channelled all my passion into you."

"So how long was it going to be before you married Adrienne Alleman?" she found herself asking.

There was another pause, then his voice became deep and ironic. "I was never going to marry her, Suzannah. With Adrienne marriage wasn't on the agenda. She knew that."

"Then what is the source of her intense jealousy?" she challenged.

"Her own nature, I suppose. Jealousy is as primal as the sea. Adrienne and I had an arrangement. I thought she was handling it well. Obviously I was wrong. She read far more into it than was ever said."

"That's all it is?" she asked with more scepticism than she intended.

"You're the only woman I've ever wanted to marry, Suzannah," he returned bluntly. "The woman I am going to marry," he added. "I hope you understand that perfectly. As to the other, don't say anything more about the situation until we've had a chance to discuss it thoroughly. You can safely leave Adrienne to me. I'm fairly certain I can make her see the error of her ways."

"I hope this doesn't involve getting into bed with her?" Though she kept her tone light it was like an oil slick over deep water.

His answer came instantly, intensely. "Making love to you precludes the possibility of ever turning to another woman. Can you doubt it after our night together?"

Her whole body flushed with the memory. The crest after crest of arousal, the energy, the mystery, the passion, the illusion that they were one human being.

"The world is only real to me when you're in it, Suzannah," he said.

She closed her eyes as his words poured like a symphony into her body. "Charley loved you on sight," she said dreamily. "There was something quite extraordinary about it."

"Why not? Children perceive things in a way almost lost to us adults. I am her father. There's going to be pain attached to making that fact known but we'll all live through it and hopefully become stronger. I promise you I'll be with you both Friday evening. I won't let anything get in my way."

# CHAPTER NINE

THE sun-drenched fields were full of mares and foals; one of the most beautiful sights in the world.

"Looks like a painting come to life, doesn't it?" Nick said, looking out at the lush pastureland crisscrossed with miles of pristine white fencing.

"How many horses are we going to buy here, Nick?" Charley asked excitedly from the back seat of the Jaguar. "Oh, I love the feel of horse farms, don't you? I love all the green paddocks and the white rails." Her iridescent eyes were wide with enchantment.

"Beautiful," Nick said, nodding in agreement with his daughter's sentiments. "Your mother and I have agreed on thirty in all. Not as many as Bellemont used to stable. Quiet, obedient horses for the children. We'll get them some place else. Tom McGovern owns this place. He was once a famous jockey."

"Yes, I know," Charley answered, moving closer to the window so she could see out. "The name of the place is Greenfields. Mummy said the French doors on the house are painted Mr McGovern's old racing colours. Devil's Blue." As she was speaking a mare and its yearling broke away from their companions to gallop to the white fence, the mare putting her beautiful sculptured head over it, bobbing a greeting. "Isn't she lovely!" Eagerness and enthusiasm tripped off Charley's tongue. "Bright as a jewel. Say, that's another good name for a pony, Jewel. Lucy and I are having a competition to see who can think up the most names. The best names."

"Here's to the winner!" A smile spread over Nick's handsome mouth.

"I told Tom we'd be arriving at eleven. We're right on the dot," Suzannah said almost dreamily as she consulted the clock on the dash.

"Fine." Without thought Nick put out his hand and stroked Suzannah's cheek, a naked little touch of desire, forgetting momentarily that Charley was there, so intense was his pleasure in her mother. Suzannah was wearing narrow-legged pink linen slacks with a little clingy white top that showed her delicate breasts beneath, a simple enough outfit yet she made it look incredibly sexy and chic. She caught the flash in his eyes and she turned away, a rose flush in her cheeks. Between them shimmered a wordless sensuality, fuelled by the consummation of their love.

Tom McGovern himself greeted them in the courtyard. Sixtyish, blue polo shirt, jodhpurs, a worn peaked cap pulled down over his balding head, a stable cat curling around his foot. He raised a hand in a gesture of salute as the Jaguar drew to a halt.

"Mornin', folks." He lifted a finger to tap his cap. "Morning, little lady," he said to Charley. "Goodness, haven't you grown since I last saw you. Why she would have been..."

"Around eighteen months old, Tom," Suzannah smiled. "Say hello, Charlotte."

Charlotte obliged, giving Tom McGovern the full benefit of her sweet-tempered smile. "It was just lovely driving in, Mr McGovern," she confided in her light musical child's voice. "A mare and her yearling came over to greet us. The mare's coat was so bright it was nearly gold."

"That would be Solar Princess, out of Solar Gold by

King Darium." Tom nodded his head. "Nice breed, that one, and pricey." He turned back to Suzannah and winked.

"You remember, Nick, don't you Tom?" Suzannah asked.

"Of course I do." The two men shook hands. "You're the superstar now, son," Tom said admiringly. "I've been following your exploits in the papers. Computers, eh? The way of the future."

"Believe it, Tom." Nick smiled. "You look well."

"Life has been good to me."

"Very good indeed by the look it," Nick said, turning his dark head to look around the fine estate. "What have you lined up to show us? Charlotte is so excited she can't wait to see the horses."

"Some downright beauties." Tom ruffled Charley's glossy head. "One cussed bloke called Diablo. Not for nuthin'. He'd make a great jumper in the right hands. Yours, Suzannah. You've got a natural seat and a special way with a rogue. If you hang on a moment I'll get Paddy and young Neville to parade them around the ring. Suzannah said you'd want around twenty, Nick?"

"We figured that would be enough for the moment," Nick said.

"I really want to fix you up," said Tom. "All of these horses, with the exception of Diablo, are just what you need. Course there aren't any guarantees with horses as you well know. Know a guy who spent a million dollars on a yearling six years ago and the damned thing is the worst jumper you've ever seen. Didn't get it from me, though."

It was an exhilarating time. A time of pure delight. One horse after the other passed through the ring, some walking sedately, others at a springy trot, to be examined and assessed before being led away. Charley had he opinion about each one, not at all backward in expressing it, feet on the rails, raising herself high, with Nick's protective arm behind her.

She's like me as I was as a girl. Living and breathing horses, Suzannah thought, smiling at her daughter's pleasure. How good Nick was with her. Martin never had been a father figure. Nick had moved in right under Charley's heart.

In the end they chose eighteen horses in all, five- and six-year-olds, ex-racehorses, three ex–show horses, on young horse Suzannah fell in love with on sight, a pure black colt. "Can I ride him?" Charley begged.

"No, darling you can not," Suzannah said firmly. "A horse like this is much too big and strong for you. One day certainly. Until then Lady will do very nicely."

Charley sang in the car on the way back to Bellemont her high spirits so infectious Suzannah and Nick found themselves joining in Charley's choice of Christmas carols. She was just finishing off "O Christmas Tree" when she asked, "Who put up the first Christmas tree, anyway Was it Saint Nicholas?"

"As a matter of fact it was Martin Luther," Nick told her. "Do you know who he was?"

"I bet he was an American," Charley said. "The have great ideas."

Nick shook his head laughing. "They sure do, but th gentleman I'm talking about was a great preacher wh was born in Germany over five hundred years ago. No only was he the leader of a religious movement called the Reformation, which split Roman Catholics an Protestants, with his translation of the Bible into German but he almost single-handedly created the moder

German language. He is said to be the most influential German who has ever lived."

"And he thought up something lovely and simple like the Christmas tree?" Charley said, in admiration. "He must have been a really nice man."

"And a musician like you. The story goes one starry night when he was returning to home he looked up to the heavens and saw a brilliant formation of diamonds in the sky. It took the shape of a pyramid-shaped tree. When he got home he tried to recreate what he saw for his family and came up with the idea of a tree decorated with candles."

"Goodness, wasn't that clever," said Charley.

Nick nodded. "The idea of the Christmas tree didn't really catch on in England until hundreds of years later when Queen Victoria's husband, Prince Albert, had a Christmas tree erected every year to remind him of his German homeland. After that the ritual of the Christmas tree spread like wildfire to America and all parts of the Western World."

"You tell wonderful stories, Nick," Charley said, impressed.

"You're wonderful to tell them to. I have another surprise coming up for you."

"You do?" Charley's delicate eyebrows shot up.

"You have to be patient." He caught her smiling eyes in the rear vision.

They arrived at Nick's "surprise" as they were approaching the outskirts of Ashbury. Past avocado and macadamia nut plantations, lush farms, the big acreage properties of the well-to-do with their rambling homesteads, extensive gardens and horse paddocks. Finally the Jaguar turned into a siding moving smoothly down a red earth track baked terra cotta by the summer sun, until it pulled up outside a white-painted bungalow hung with green shutters. The timber banisters of the verandah were smothered with the brightest blue morning glories, like a fantastic curtain, and violet and emerald butterflies danced across its dazzling surface. The house was deserted. Mosses and ferns clung to every rung of the short flight of steps, the rampant vine interweaving with the lacy branches of an overhead tree. There was such a silence, a stillness about it, it might have been a house in a fairytale.

"There's no one home," Charley announced in a hushed voice. "But I think there's someone watching us."

Suzannah shivered, seeing a figure up there on the verandah waving. "Don't be silly, darling. Are we going in, Nick?" She turned her face and her body towards him, her emotions breaking through at the story of their lives.

"Let's!" Charley, all innocence, was already moving to open the door. "This is where you lived, Nick, isn't it? I can tell. I *love* it that you brought me."

"Stop her, Nick," Suzannah urged, her fingers pressed to her lips.

"What's the matter, darling?" Nick asked in a startlingly tender voice.

"Too many memories." She put her face into her hands.

But Charley was already darting through the broken-hinged white timber gate.

"It's all right. We'll be together," Nick reassured her, sliding out of the car and coming around to her. "Charlotte, wait for us," he called.

Trembling a little, Suzannah took Nick's hand. "Back

to the beginning," she said. "Back to where it all began."

"We're powerless to lose the past, Suzannah," he said quietly. "Come with me now. There's nothing to fear. There's no one here now but gentle ghosts."

Charley was standing perfectly still like a child in the middle of a magic circle, looking around her, breathing in the scent of a thicket of blossoming old rosebushes that had survived neglect and the passage of time. A luminous gold-green light bathed her small figure and painted the creamy beauty of her young skin. "Isn't it sweet?" she said. "Sweet and mysterious like an illustration in a storybook. And so small! How did you fit in there, Nick?" She stared back at his powerful, lean height.

"I just did." He smiled, coming up to her, ruffling her hair. "Not everyone grows up in a mansion like Bellemont."

"Do you suppose we can go inside?" she asked. Her hair had escaped its loose pigtail and long curls fell on either side of her cheeks.

"It would be shut, wouldn't it, Nick?" Suzannah found herself leaning against him and unconsciously he slid a supporting arm around her waist, a gesture full of meaning that Charley took note of.

"Don't you want to go in, Mummy?" she asked, profoundly startled the way her mother was clinging to Nick as though she'd be content to stay there forever. Startled but utterly pleased.

"Why don't we see?" Nick led the way up onto the verandah, while Charley ran off along the side, rapping on one set of doors, then the other. "So many visions of you are swirling around in my head." Nick brushed the top of Suzannah's head with his lips. "This beautiful little girl with all the pretty dresses and the hair ribbons, so full of charm, so polite, so good at her lessons she could make my parents smile as they looked at her.''

''If only I'd been older, wiser, to appreciate them better,'' Suzannah said, the dark wing of her hair falling forward on her cheek. ''They were exceptional people. I'll remember them all my life.''

''Nick, we can get in here,'' Charley's excited voice suddenly shouted.

''Just hold on,'' he called in a firm and, it had to be noted, parental tone. ''Better see what she's up to.'' Slowly he released Suzannah. ''There's no need for you to come in if you don't want to.''

''I'll be a strong, brave girl.'' She lifted her head and followed him.

''This is delicious!'' Charley was clapping her hands together, her extraordinary eyes sparkling. ''When I get home I'm going to write a story about it. Perhaps I'll be a famous author?''

''You've got enough imagination,'' Suzannah told her, watching Nick put pressure on a French door so it suddenly flew in.

All was enveloped in silence.

Suzannah had been in the small living room so many times she remembered exactly where every piece of furniture had been. The position of the upright piano beside the wall. The painting above it, a light-filled romantic landscape. Nothing dreadful happened. No overwhelming sense of sadness. She remembered where Nick's father used to sit in his special chair, his fine handsome face drawn with pain but never a word of complaint. Often he used to sit in on her piano lesson, remarking on the speed of her progress and his wife's wonderful ability to impart the wealth of knowledge and technique she had acquired through a lifetime of making music. She remembered Nick, sitting on an old rocker out on the verandah waiting for her to finish so they could go down to the river. Amazingly the old rocking chair remained and a few other pieces of wicker furniture moved in from the verandah—an old settee and two armchairs.

Charley went like an arrow to sit in the rocker, not even hearing her mother's objection. "Darling, it might be dusty."

"Leave her, Suzy," Nick said, memories of his parents weighing on his heart. "She looks just right in it."

Charley looked up to smile at them, her eyes wide and bright. "This only needs a paint."

"It does, too," Nick said.

"Could we take it with us?"

"Why?"

"Because I think I need it."

Suzannah couldn't speak for fear her voice would break but Nick answered. "I suppose we could, as it belongs to us. But I think I'll send someone to fetch it. Someone who can restore it."

"Oh, Nick, you're so good to us. What else is there?" Charley said, jumping up.

"Oh the usual thing," Nick said, beginning to make off for a quick inspection of the bungalow before Charley got started looking around. "Bedrooms of course," he called. "Kitchen, bathroom, a little sewing room, my mother's sitting room, the back porch."

"Can I go and explore?" Charley asked, as the empty rooms held wonder upon wonder.

"Go right ahead," Nick returned, casting a quick glance at the silent Suzannah, seeming to include her in his next words. "There's nothing to hurt you."

"I just might get the tiniest bit dirty," Charley said

gleefully. "One time when I was small I got stuck in the
attic at Bellemont and Mummy couldn't find me for
hours."

"Don't remind me." Suzannah shivered at the memory. She and her father had been out of their minds with
anxiety. Her father, in fact, had begun to raise the subject
of kidnapping. Even Martin had shown a deep concern
for the missing child. One of the rare times.

"She is intrigued." Nick turned to give Suzannah his
incomparable smile as Charley skipped off. "You'd think
it was Aladdin's cave."

"She's lovely. Little girl innocent," Suzannah sighed.
"I was like that once."

"I swear to God you were extraordinary." Nick
walked towards her, pulling her into his arms. "You still
are." He felt the same powerful emotional current running between them.

"When did it all start to go wrong?" The words pulsed
out.

His heart bucked like a colt's as she laid her head
gently against his chest as she had done so often in the
past. He savoured it, not bothering to hide his intensity.
She was back in his arms where she belonged.

"When your father began to hate me," he said. "Fear
me, more probably. It had nothing to do with my being
'foreign'. The fact my parents were immigrants who had
lost all their material possessions in life, their once high
standing, it had to do with war. You're right, Suzannah,
you were always the prize."

She nodded mutely, then sighed. "He was sorry at the
end."

"I know," he said quietly. "But it will take me a long
time to heal. In trying to maintain his control your father
very nearly destroyed us all. You and Martin made an

unhappy marriage that was doomed to fail. I threw myself desperately into my work, determined to become a big success. Meanwhile some of the best years of our lives ground past. My parents never lived to see their grandchild.''

Suzannah tilted her head, shifting her gaze. ''Who says they can't see her now?'' she questioned. ''I remember they really, really, believed in God.''

Surely that was true. ''I don't know what to believe any more,'' Nick said ruefully. ''All I know is the bond between us could last a thousand years.'' He lowered his dark head to drop a brief, half-tormented kiss on her upturned mouth. The pain, the pity, the disillusionment, the loss of his daughter's tender years.

At that very moment Charley returned and saw them locked together, her iridescent eyes spilling a clear message of anxiety. ''You love Mummy, don't you, Nick?'' she said, after a time.

He didn't hesitate to speak the truth. ''Yes, Charlotte, I do. I hope with all my heart that's all right with you?''

Charley stood staring, trying to sort out her thoughts; deal with her memories of a father who had never given her the love she needed. ''Are you going to try to love me?''

''Oh, darling!'' Suzannah gave a little sob that passed for a laugh while Nick went to his daughter, going down on his haunches so he could look directly into her eyes. ''Charlotte,'' he said in a deep, emotion-charged voice. ''There's not one other little girl in the entire world I would want more for a daughter than you. None in the world.''

Although Charley rallied noticeably, seeing the tears tracking down her mother's face, her voice quavered. ''You really mean that, don't you, Nick?''

"Come on," he said, drawing her into his arms and hugging her tightly. "Let me show you, my little love."

Tired out by all the excitement, Charley ate an early supper then went uncomplainingly to bed, closing her eyes as soon as her head touched the pillow. So many lovely things to dream about. So many wonderful things to do when she woke up in the morning. She felt so happy her small body couldn't contain it. Although it had never been fully explored, Charley, a highly intelligent, sensitive child, had suffered keenly from Martin's indifference. Now it was time to be exuberant with joy. She and Mummy were as close as mother and daughter could get. Now there was Nick, wonderful Nick, to love her. Charley went off to sleep on cloud nine.

There were so many faxes left for Nick that he read them through right away. He had been talking of staying on for a day or two but his pressing commitments would drag him back. They ate their evening meal in the beautiful cool of the plant-filled conservatory, a place the Sheffield family had long used as an informal dining room, then afterwards while Suzannah cleared away, Nick returned to the study to make endless phone calls and deal with the faxes more closely.

He was still at it well after nine so Suzannah decided to shampoo her hair and take her shower for the night. It had been a long, emotional day, half exhilarating, half draining. If Nick was returning to Sydney in the morning he would be up and away early. For that matter, she and Hans had an early appointment with a young man of some experience who wanted to work in the winery.

She took her time under the shower then afterwards, wrapped in a big pink bath towel, stood before the mirror drying her hair, watching it take on a high gleam as she began to brush it into its thick pageboy style. Her hair was fine but heavy, well behaved. It fell quickly into place. Charley's was developing a pronounced deep wave with the special interest of that giveaway widow's peak. It was rapidly filling in from the light, fine suggestion of her early years. Valerie had commented on it. Valerie who was going to speak quietly to her family. For all the lifetime of closeness and friendship there was bound to be at least one of them who would condemn her for what she had done. She understood and anticipated it. One paid for one's sins.

When she was finally ready to leave her bedroom, dressed in a magnolia satin nightgown, its matching robe tied tightly around her waist, it was to find Nick had finished work in the study. The light was off so she went in search of him, finding him standing out on the upstairs balcony, his two arms outstretched against the balustrade, his striking dark head lifted to the timeless beauty of the stars. The Southern Cross was directly over the house, the Milky Way, a sparkling scintillating net of dreams. It was a beautiful scene and he appeared to be absorbed in it. She thought he probably hadn't even heard her. She was wearing soft bedroom mules and her footsteps on the carpet hadn't made a sound. But just as she went to speak, he called to her without turning. "Come here to me. I need you in my arms. I need you *now*."

He turned his tall lean body slightly as she flowed towards him, putting out an arm to gather her in. "You smell wonderful!" He buried his face in her gleaming scented hair.

"You have to go back in the morning?" she asked, her body going from calm to needy longing for his.

"Nothing else for it." He rested his chin on the top

of her head. "I'm needed. Now and again Konrads turns into a one-man band."

"What time?" She relaxed her body into his. How she drew on his strength. His energy!

"I'll get away around six. No need for you to get up. You'll have to say my goodbyes to Charlotte. We have to resolve this situation swiftly, Suzannah, difficult as it is. We must tell her. Small she may be but she has a right to know, otherwise she'll feel cheated by the people who are closest to her in all the world. That's you and me, Suzannah. Charlotte's parents."

Suzannah waited a moment, then looked up. "You never did tell me what you said to Adrienne?"

He framed her face with his hands. "I let her see that spreading scandal can work two ways. In her public relations business one needs to stay on good terms with valuable connections. Adrienne is a success in her own right but her business might quickly fold if I started to spread the word she was a dangerous woman to cross."

"But would you do it?" Suzannah asked, doubtfully. "I've never seen you do a vindictive thing."

He gave a low laugh like a growl. "I can be as ruthless as the next one, Suzannah, if the people I love are threatened. I think you'll find when you next speak to Valerie White, Adrienne never sent any letter."

"Oh, I hope not," she murmured. "It would be dreadfully unfair. Valerie has suffered enough."

"I'm hoping to put an end to it. Let's sit down." He drew her back towards a long rattan sofa, plushly upholstered in white cotton. "We have to plan our next moves." Nick settled into one end but as Suzannah began to curl up beside him, tucking her feet under her, he quickly manoeuvred her slender body so she half lay across him, her head in his lap. "That's better," he sighed.

"Things could become unpleasant, Nick," she warned him, looking up into his face. "We would have to be prepared for it."

"Where are you expecting the main unpleasantness to come from?" he asked.

"Oh..." She put up her hands and he caught them, carrying them to his mouth. "Martin's family. Valerie is a remarkable woman but the others mightn't have her wisdom and understanding. Losing a husband and son, Valerie knows all about suffering. She knows what is and what isn't truly important in life."

"So there'll be talk?" Nick sounded like a man no one would mess with. "Wrongs don't make a right. Charlotte must know who her real father is. We're going to give her all the love and support that she needs. People with eyes in their head must have started to take note she has a look of me even if they don't remember my mother. The whole town remembers what went on at the time.

"Of course it will cause a lot of talk. Another nine-day wonder. I'm counting on people's acceptance. I'm counting on their affection for you and for Charlotte. As for me, the contribution I'm going to make to the district should help."

"How I wish it could be as easy as that!"

"It *must* be so, Suzannah. We're going to make it so," Nick said urgently, his hand sweeping from the curve of her chin, down the line of her throat, across her satin-clad shoulder to claim her breast. "I only want to do what is good and right. I don't want the bad times any more. Do you have a problem with that?"

She felt compelled to voice it. "I have a problem with that part of you that blames me for much of what hap-

pened. I know now I should have defied my father, I
should have made your mother listen to me. I should have
made her tell me where you had gone. I should have
overcome my fears. I had betrayed you so terribly you
wouldn't want to see me.''

''We have to leave all that behind, Suzannah,'' he said,
feeling her heart racing under his caressing hand.

''Can we?''

''You're the fever in my blood,'' he told her, his eyes
as black as midnight.

''I wonder if you don't actually hate me in some little
way?'' she persisted, trying to get it all straight.

''Hate is the road to ruin.'' He gave a dark half laugh,
slipping his hand under the warm satin, finding her naked
flesh.

His touch was exquisite, now rimming the blossoming
nipple, teasing it to a tight bud. She didn't resist as he
slipped the robe from her shoulders. ''You missed the
night Charley was born,'' she said, sounding young and
terribly vulnerable. ''I could only think to bite my tongue
not to call out for you. I remember the awful pain, then
finally, long after, a very small bundle being placed on
my breast. I adored her from that moment. I looked
around everywhere for you but you weren't there.''

''Don't.'' He felt the anguish. Knew the pain.

''You weren't there, either, when she said her first
words. You weren't there to catch her when she took her
first steps, arms outstretched. You weren't there for her
first day at school. My fault.''

''What on earth are you trying to do to me?'' He had
trouble not inflicting torturous rapture on her body. As it
was he lifted her to him, a steely hand at her back.

''I want to know if you hate me for that?'' she challenged, making no attempt to break free. "Don't tell me any comforting lies, either."

"Well then I hate you," he said in a harsh voice. "Love you. Love you like no one else in the world. You *know* you hurt me terribly but do you think I'm so cruel I can't weep tears for you? Stop this insane self-recrimination, Suzannah. Stop it right now before I snap. I'm your husband in my own eyes. Soon in the eyes of the world. Every big decision brings a new set of problems. The whole idea is to find a solution."

"And one of your solutions is making love?"

He gave an angry laugh. "The way I see it your body was made for me. Are you going to tell me any different?"

"No." As always her love for him swept her away. No one had Nick's intensity. He gathered her up almost violently, coming to his feet, holding her high, the outline of his tall figure flaring in the light from the bedroom like the areola around the sun.

She turned up a rapt face to him, bones melting, heart swelling, blood turned to honey. "We're going to have a future," she repeated. "A wonderful future."

"Tell me you're mine." He turned a deliberate half circle so the light fell directly on her face like a spotlight.

"I love you," she said in a worshipping voice, feeling their shared desire like a pulsing electric current. "All the happiness in life depends on you."

That admission brought his mouth down on hers in a kiss that dizzied her with intense pleasure. The glory of being wanted! The glory of returning such glowing desire.

Nick moved then, full of an absolute elation, carrying her swiftly into the bedroom, placing her like a flower to bloom across his bed.

His vision was whole for him now. Suzannah, himself and their child. A universe of three.

Some days later, with Nick back in Sydney, Suzannah and Charley took their Christmas lists into town. They'd had long discussions over which gifts would best please, now they were out to purchase them. They visited shop after shop, Charley in high good humour, Suzannah catching her first true sense of Christmas. By midday they were laden down with parcels and had to return to the car to leave them before they went on to lunch at Suzannah's favourite small restaurant, which welcomed children.

"Christmas has to be the most wonderful time of the year!" Charley said blissfully, glancing around the riverside restaurant with its sparkling Christmas tree in the foyer, tiny silver Christmas trees decorating the tables and sumptuous red, green and gold swags around the walls. "The room is full of people. We know most of them." She put up a hand to wave at one of her school friends sitting with her mother and grandmother at a nearby table.

Suzannah, too, turned to smile and the others waved back. "I expect they've all been doing their Christmas shopping like us. Now, my pet, what are you going to have?"

"A lemonade to start." Charley bowed her head over the menu. "Then maybe chicken and chips. I like it in the basket. Then if I've got any room left, could I please have some mud cake?"

"We'll see." Suzannah started to smile. It wasn't much good plying Charley with food. She wasn't a big eater. She usually had trouble finishing her main course.

That day, however, she ate with gusto, keeping up a

flow of conversation that warmed Suzannah's heart. Charley was a vivid child and, for one so young, she had a wide range of interests. She might as well have been having lunch with an entertaining young adult. Before Nick had gone back to Sydney they had agreed to tell Charley the whole truth surrounding her birth. They would pick the right time and the setting. They would explain it to her as delicately and gently as they knew how, knowing full well there would be a degree of upset in the news...but above all an affirmation of their love for her. Her father had returned to claim her. He would never have left her, only he didn't know. Charley was possessed of intelligence and understanding. They had to rely on it.

They weren't home ten minutes before a car pulled into the driveway, stopping near the front steps.

"It's Aunty Nicole." Charley, standing in the middle of the hallway, called out to her mother. "She's by herself. What a shame!"

That brought Suzannah hurrying down the staircase, her hand tight on the banister. Had Valerie told her story? The answer most likely was yes. It was quite possible Nicole had come to have it out with her. But never in front of Charley.

Nicole swept into the entrance hall, looking like a woman under a great deal of pressure. "Hello, Charley," she said without her usual gentle touch on the child's arm or her shoulder. "Suzannah, may I have a word with you?"

"Of course." Suzannah's nerves tightened. "Are you alone? You didn't bring the children?"

"Well, I asked them to remain in the car." Nicole's eyes were overbright, almost glazed, and her cheeks were flushed. "We have lots to do. This will only take a few moments."

"Oh good! I'll go out and speak to them," Charley called, running happily from the house.

Interpreting Suzannah's anxious expression, Nicole said bitterly, "Don't worry, they don't know. Not *yet!*"

Suzannah put out a hand indicating they should go into the drawing room. "I take it Valerie has spoken to you?"

"I had the sensation the floor was going to come up and hit me," Nicole said, anger and shock thick in her throat. "Suzannah, how could you? You've always been up there so high in my mind. You're so beautiful, so good, my kids love you, now this! You're going to humiliate us all."

Suzannah brushed that aside. "There's plenty of humiliation in life, Nicole," Suzannah said. "I'm profoundly sorry to have to hurt the family, but it's time I told the truth. Charley has to know. Nick wants his chance to be a father. He loves Charley already. And she loves him. It's as if at some level she *knows*."

"And what about my kids?" Nicole demanded, slumping into an armchair. "Don't you think they're going to be shocked out of their minds? Charley is their cousin. They've grown up with that. Now she isn't. I'm not her aunt. Neither is Kate. Wait until she finds out! Mum has lost a grandchild. I'm just so sick and shocked."

Suzannah nodded in understanding. "Forgive me, Nicole. That's all I can ask. It's all my fault. I accept the full blame. It's not what I wanted, believe me."

"You didn't want Martin." Nicole's eyes misted over.

"I tried to be a good wife to him, Nicole. Don't try to take that away from me," Suzannah said quietly. "I meant to make my marriage work."

Nicole was silent, forced to acknowledge it. She sat on the very edge of her chair. "And what about the town?"

Suzannah clicked her tongue. "Stop worrying about the town, Nicole. Nick and I are an old story. The town will talk for a while but they'll adjust. It's the family I'm concerned about. The effect on Charley when we tell her."

"God!" Nicole was trying to think through layers and layers of consequences. "I know it's tough, Suzy. I even know Martin and your father did a bad thing. But hell! I *love* Charley."

"Why not! She loves you." Suzannah reached out and grasped Nicole's hand. "Don't let this ruin everything, Nicole. We're all the same people. We all care about one another. I've always called you family and you're still family. Don't cut Charley off. She's only a little girl with her whole life in front of her. Don't ruin her relationship with the children. When you speak to them I want you to be very kind. Kind and forgiving."

"Hell, why am I so mean?" Nicole gasped. "It's just that I can't take it in, when Mum *knew*."

"Martin always spoke to his mother. He always confided in her," Suzannah explained.

"God, aren't I a fool. And blind. I always thought Charley was the image of you. Maybe she hasn't got your eyes but everything else. Now I can see the resemblance to Nick. How long has he known?"

"Since he first laid eyes on her," Suzannah said, simply.

"How did he deal with it?" Nicole asked.

"Much better that I dared hope. The guilt has been terrible, Nicole. I've suffered. I suppose the suffering will never stop."

Nicole cringed. "It has to if we can all escape the shame."

Suzannah rejected that. "No shame, Nicole. That's a word I won't have any part of. I'm very proud of Charley. And of Nick. What happened, happened."

"Turning Martin into an alcoholic," Nicole offered bleakly.

Suzannah shook her head, knowing it was true. "Martin had his own problems, Nicole. You think back about that. He wouldn't allow himself to be happy. *I* want another chance."

"So you're going to marry Nick." It was acceptance not a question.

Suzannah nodded. "In time. Next year. If he hadn't been driven away, if I hadn't given in to so much pressure, we would have been married long ago."

Nicole got up slowly from her chair. "I guess so. I always thought you were meant for each other. Just give me a little time with this, Suzy. Why isn't life ever simple?" she turned to ask.

"Because human beings aren't simple." Tears sprang to Suzannah's eyes from her own wounded place. "Just remember you're all very important to me. You've played a big part in my life. I don't want that to stop."

Inside the car Charley tried desperately to control her shock and confusion, the anger that made her want for the first time in her life to fight with her cousins. Only they weren't her cousins any longer. Pride kept the tears from her eyes.

"And don't you tell Mummy, either," Lucy warned. "We weren't supposed to hear."

"No, Mummy would be terribly angry," Laura said. "She and Nanna were talking in private. They didn't realise we were outside the door. I feel ashamed now. We stood there listening.

"Oh Charley," Laura wailed. "Now you're not our cousin we mightn't be able to play with you."

"I don't *want* to play with you." Lucy, childlike, lashed out from the depths of her own upset. Charley had always been her cousin. Now she was some other person. Not even Uncle Martin's child. She felt too dizzy to go shopping. She felt hurt and angry.

In spite of their fraught feelings all three children managed to act normal when Nicole came out. Charley slipped quickly out of the car and ran past Nicole, offering a polite goodbye, without stopping. What should she do? Where should she go? She had to think all this out for herself. It was impossible to be angry with her mother. She loved her mother so much. She was amazed to hear from Lucy that Nick was her father. Nick! No wonder he had said he would pick her for a daughter in all the world. She *was* his daughter. It was amazing. His mother had been her grandmother. Not Nanna White. So many thoughts pressed down on her head. Why hadn't they told her? Did they think because she was a little kid she didn't need to know? No, that couldn't be right. She and Mummy had lots of long conversations about lots of grown-up things. Why was it such a terrible secret? Were they ashamed of her? That wasn't right, either. It had something to do with Mummy being married to the man she had called "Daddy". The daddy who couldn't bring himself to love her.

Charley felt overwhelmed. In a mess. She remembered now she always felt good when she worked out solutions in maths. She would go off and find a safe place where she could work this whole thing out by herself.

\* \* \*

It was getting on towards dusk before Suzannah returned to the house, carrying a basketful of luscious table grapes Kurt Schroeder had picked for her.

"Charley," she called out. "I'm back." She thought Charley would come running. She had left Charley in her room watching a new video that would run for over an hour. Plenty of staff were working in close proximity to the house so she was quite safe.

After a few moments she realised Charley wasn't coming. Probably she hadn't heard her. Suzannah left the basket of grapes in the kitchen then walked up the stairs to Charley's room, surprised no sound of the video was coming from it. Surely the movie wasn't over? She had checked on the running time.

When she found the room empty Suzannah's face blanched. She had never really gotten over the fright of the experience in the attic. "Charley," she called. "Charley." Her daughter had grown out of playing hide-and-seek. She didn't like to make Suzannah anxious.

The house was so large. Too large it now seemed. Suzannah flew around in an increasing panic, calling her daughter's name as she went. Finally convinced Charley wasn't anywhere in the house she ran out into the grounds calling to the staff who were working on, oblivious to any trouble.

Hans was the first one to answer, coming in from the rose garden, stripping off his gloves.

"What is it, Suzannah?" He knew panic when he heard it.

"I can't find Charley anywhere." Suzannah wrung her hands. "She was in the house watching a video when I left. It's only been an hour."

"You've searched the house thoroughly?" Hans asked, his thick brows working.

"Yes. She's not there."

"Right, we search the grounds, the stables." He turned away immediately to organise the men.

"The stables, oh!" Suzannah felt a ray of hope. "She could be there." On the other hand Charley would never attempt to ride without permission.

Night fell and Charley still wasn't found. Nick answered his phone at the third ring, his heart rocking as Suzannah, sounding distraught, gave him the news.

"Did something happen to upset her?" he asked, already seeking out a phone contact.

"No," Suzannah answered, her conviction fading as she gave the question more thought. "Nicole was here," she said. "She came to see me but the children didn't know."

"Children have a way of finding out everything," Nick said grimly.

"Get onto Harris."

"I already have." Suzannah made a valiant attempt to pull herself together. "The whole town has turned out to search. Oh, Nick, come quickly."

He flew in by helicopter, landing on Bellemont's front lawn where a command post had been hastily set up. The news of Charley's disappearance had raised enormous concerns. Nothing like this ever happened in the district. Everyone knew Nick Konrads was a rich man. Suzannah and the child were living at the house. Was there a connection?

Inside the house Nick found Suzannah trying to comfort her sister-in-law, Nicole, when he thought it should have been the other way round.

"Suzannah?"

She went to him and he drew her into his arms, lovingly, protectively, a rock of strength, feeling the trem-

bling that ran right through her body. "Nicole has jus
told me the children knew," Suzannah told him. "They'
been listening outside the door when she and her mothe
were talking."

"And they told Charlotte?" Nick's black eyes cam
to rest on Nicole's bent blond head. She looked a small
despairing figure.

"I'm afraid so." Suzannah shuddered. "But Charle
said nothing. Nothing at all. She seemed a little preoc
cupied that's all. I thought she was thinking about wha
to say on her Christmas cards. She's like that. I left he
watching a video. I was only gone an hour. She too
Lady."

"Without permission?" Nick was surprised.

"She must have had a good reason, Nick," Suzanna
said. "She must have wanted to get away by herself."

Nicole came over, tried to explain, but Nick put he
aside gently. "Has anyone tried the bungalow?" h
asked.

"Your parents' place?" Suzannah's heart did a som
ersault. "I don't know. I wouldn't think so. It wasn'
mentioned."

"Then I think we should try there," Nick said. Th
idea simply sprang out. "Where's your car?"

"Take mine, please," Nicole pleaded. "It's in th
drive. The keys are in it. I'll never forgive myself
something has happened to Charley. Neither will th
girls."

Along the route they could see the search parties i
the woods and fields, grateful beyond words for the com
munity support.

The bungalow was in total darkness. Just a shape. Th
electricity had long since been cut off but when Nick an
Suzannah broke into the house, they heard to their grea

relief and joy Charley's startled cry, then a tremulous "Who's there?" It was better than the voice of angels.

"It's me!" Suzannah shouted, walking into a chair. "It's Mummy, darling. Nick is with me. Oh, Charley, where are you?"

Nick flashed his torch, going ahead. It lit up his daughter's small figure standing near the back door. He moved swiftly towards her, calling, "Sweetheart, sweetheart," an immense gratitude in his heart. She seemed perfectly all right.

"Charlotte, you've given us all such a terrible fright!" His arms closed around her as he lifted her off the ground.

"I'm so sorry," she said, laying her dark head on his shoulder. "I'm so sorry, Daddy."

Later when she was safely home in bed and the search parties had been called off—Nick promised the town would be properly thanked—Charley told them all about it. "I wanted to think it all out by myself. I knew you wouldn't let me take Lady out, Mummy, and I'm sorry, but I needed her to get to my grandparents' house. I knew it was the right place to be. I know now why Daddy showed me."

"How wonderful you can call me that." Nick bent tenderly over his child, smoothing back her dark hair.

She smiled up at him, the very picture of angelic childhood innocence. "I dreamed you might become my daddy. Now it's true. I thought so hard I fell asleep on the floor. When I woke up it was really dark. Darker than any place I've ever been and the wind was blowing through all the cracks in the doors. But I wasn't afraid, I thought someone really kind was with me. I wasn't game to try to ride Lady home because there wasn't any moon, so I decided to stay until morning.''

"Oh God!" Suzannah murmured.

"I'm sorry, Mummy. Did you have an awful time?" Charley immediately looked contrite.

"I was very worried, Charley," Suzannah said. "I rang your father straight away. He arrived in a helicopter.''

"Truly?" Charley's eyes opened wide. "Is it still here?"

"No." Nick moved off the edge of the bed and stood up to go to Suzannah. "But I can always organise a ride.''

"How do you really feel about the news, Charlotte?" he asked. "You must tell us. Your mother and I fully intended to tell you, when I returned at the weekend. We're both very sorry it turned out differently. Nicole's little girls were terribly upset when they thought you were missing. They love you and they want to see you tomorrow.''

"Dear Lucy, dear Laura. I'm not mad at them any more. They can help us wrap the presents, can't they, Mummy?''

"All except their own. So all's well that ends well, Charley?" Suzannah looked deeply into her daughter's eyes, as Nick's arm slipped around her waist, drawing her to him.

"This is going to be the best Christmas ever!" said Charley.